THE PHOTO OP

A novel by William E. Chisham

The Photo Op

Published By:
Old Red Barn Publishing
P.O. Box 921
Sequim, WA 98382, USA

Cataloging-in-Publication Data is on file with the Library of Congress.

Library of Congress Control Number: 2008908365

ISBN 978-0-615-20245-7

Produced in the United States of America

September 2008

First Edition

Soft cover

Also by the Author:

"Reflexions,": 1985-86
A Poetry Chapbook
1986

"The Road North -
Tales of an Urban Sourdough"
2007

"Habitatin' for Humanity"
2008

Dedication

In memory of Herb Jaenicke and Paul Emerson for their many years of dedicated effort in maintaining and improving the Juneau trail system. Wherever they are now, Paul at eighty-plus is probably in the lead on the trail. Thanks to the many volunteers who have shown up at work parties to do trail bushing and maintenance, giving new life to Juneau area trails. And special thanks to my wife, Kay, for sharing years of speculation about a roll of film envisioned during a San Diego vacation.

Table of Contents

Photo Opportunity, i.e. Photo Op

photo opportunity n A brief period reserved for the press to photograph the participants in a newsworthy event. The American Heritage College Dictionary, Fourth Edition. Copyright 2004, Houghton Mifflin Company.

"Which would imply that members of the press are expected to be present and that photographs will be taken. An event or happening at other times which might be equally newsworthy although a member or members of the press are not expected to be present may arguably also be a photo op. This, of course, leads to issues such as a reasonable expectation of privacy in your home or hotel room even if you are a public figure at the top of the food chain. Not to mention national security issues. The simple answer is to not at any time or place engage in any conduct that you would not want seen on the evening news. But, being human...." Lectures On Ethics Of Responsible Journalism, Moldenhauer, 1994.

THE PHOTO OP

THE SATURDAY HIKE

I suppose that the whole thing - the seemingly impossible yet interlocked cascade of far and near events - might never have involved me if I had not helped set up a volunteer group to help maintain hiking trails in the valleys and mountains around our town in Southeast Alaska. However, the group was established, our volunteers worked on keeping up area trails, and I found a hidden journal telling of a fearful pursuit unfolding around us.

Our group, Trail Fixers, had been approached by a guy from the Forest Service about two metal huts high on a ridge a few miles south of town. Being on federal land and no longer used, the Corps of Engineers was trying to 'give' them to the Forest Service for recreational shelters. The fact that there was no really usable trail leading to them had caused that agency to ask if we would maintain a new trail if one was built. Our group agreed to hike up and see whether it was a project we might want to be involved in. Knowing how long federal agencies can take to proceed from concept to plan to approval to budget to scheduling to doing did not make us feel that the project was on a priority basis. At least it would be a nice hike over different terrain.

In early June of that year, after most of the snow was gone from the alpine areas above the tree line, Dave, Paul, Herb and I made plans to hike up early on a Saturday morning to see if we wanted to agree to help keep up a new trail when and if one was ever built. Doing that in exchange for the occasional weekend use i.e. hunting season, of a shelter in remote terrain had some appeal to a few of us anyway.

The day promised to be ideal as it followed one of the rare two-day dry spells Juneau has once or twice every summer. We had agreed to meet for an early fueling-up breakfast at the Viking on Front Street before heading about five miles out Thane Road to the Sheep Creek Trailhead. It was a typical post-Friday-night morning downtown with only a few of the regulars still standing outside the Triangle Club and the Rendezvous. It would be a few hours before the cruise ships started to fill the street with crowds of tourists seeking a real Alaska experience as they shopped at places like Little Switzerland and Uncle Artie's T-Shirt Shop for treasures not made in this state or country, but which were at least 'from their Alaska adventure.'

After filling up on items not found on the current Food Pyramid and enough coffee to make us glad that we would be outdoors, it was time to head out. With daypacks on, we crossed the wet planks over the ditch by the parking lot and headed up the only straight part of the trail. Every trail around Juneau seems either to be down a steep path to a beach or up a long winding slope replete with switchbacks, and is either muddy, rocky or all of the above. This one met all those requirements with a few more challenges tossed in to make it more interesting. The sound of water cascading down an unseen creek was background music to our progress. We managed to reach the top of the hill in about thirty minutes of steady hiking to where the trail descended into the

Sheep Creek Valley. The trail down into the valley was almost invisible in the bright green background. After a short break to catch our breath and to savor the view across the valley we headed down the slope. The trail wound along the valley floor next to the creek, past the back side of the long silent A J Mine and a few decaying wooden buildings leaning into history. The almost level trail ended as we reached the far side of the valley.

The next part of the hike up, after leaving the nearest somewhat brushed trail, was up and around the many switchbacks that helped on the ascent while we contended with eroded spots hidden by brush and our world-class Devil's Club. The hike quickly became an endurance march as we battled the brush, rocks, and slide areas while climbing steadily for over an hour to make the 300 to 500 feet gain in elevation up to Power Line Ridge. Occasionally we would cross the last remnants of winter snow. Marmots whistled from the rocks around us as they scurried around on marmot errands. Sun, a rare visitor to these parts, beat down on us while encouraging hoards of insects camped out waiting for unwary hikers to show patches of winter-whitened skin as offerings to them. I went several rounds with the deer flies and well-armed mosquitoes that seemed to enjoy the bug dope I had resorted to before finally conceding to the attackers.

At last we came to the tree line and crossed the heather-covered meadows to where the first hut was located. We took a break at the top of the ridge to enjoy the fantastic view south down the channel toward Taku Inlet, took some photos of the hut inside and out, and hiked on to the second hut about a mile further on.

The huts, as it turned out, weren't really huts but shelters made from very large diameter culvert pipes with the lower third buried below ground level. That, plus heavy steel cable tie downs, kept the huts in place during winter winds that sometimes roared past at speeds in excess of two hundred miles an hour on the ridge. At lower elevations these become the Taku winds that can chill and bend even the hardiest local trying to walk around downtown Juneau.

How the pipes were hauled up to this elevation is a mystery that may rank with how the pyramids were built or who made the figures on Easter Island. The pipes were made into shelters by the use of wood-framed plywood ends and a door beefed up with heavy lumber. A roof exit allowed occupants to get out when snow covered the shelter and lower door. The idea was to provide a place for work and as emergency shelters for power line crews working in the remote area years earlier bringing more power to our town.

When experience and practicality were later added to engineering knowledge, the line was rerouted to a lower area marginally less prone to avalanche damage.

The shelters were then abandoned by the power agency and left to rust and rot over the seasons. More recently, the shelters had been used by guys from the Bureau of Mines when they needed to wait out bad weather while researching mining history in the area.

Sudden weather changes are not unknown around Juneau.

After taking more pictures, we entered the shelter through the rough wooden door which was still upright on rusty hinges that could have used a liberal dose of WD-40. Our flashlights were needed to light up the gloomy, musty interior. A rough set of dust-covered wooden shelves clung tenaciously to the back wall with a few worn pans and cooking utensils rusting on them. Two worn work boots with laces entwined hung from one end of the shelving. Food and beer cans graced the remains of plywood sheets covering the dirt floor. The other guys, having had enough of this rustic mountain shelter splendor, soon wandered back outside for fresher air and to discuss the prospects of hikers renting windowless places such as these for weekend solitude after packing in food, fuel, and water.

I was headed for the door to join the others when my boot caught on a rotting corner of the flooring, knocking a piece loose. So much for a dry deck to rest on. Then my flashlight beam focused on something under the place where the plywood had been. As I bent over and brushed away a layer of dirt and rotted wood, I saw what appeared to be the corner of a leather-bound journal. After carefully lifting it out, I placed it in a plastic trash bag from my daypack to look at later. I replaced the loose flooring and hurried outside to catch up with the others, who had already started across the meadows on the trek down the ridge and back to town.

Just as I stepped out and pushed the heavy door closed, a helicopter suddenly passed overhead, wheeled around, and made a low pass over us before flying back in the direction of our distant local airport. That, looking back, was the first clue that something was going on with the shelter site.

The second omen was that the chopper was not from either of our local flying services and did not have Coast Guard or National Guard markings. I, of course did not think of them as omens yet.

I might not have even given the flyover or unrecognized markings much thought as we started down past the tree line except that as we finally got back to the main trail, another party of three hikers were headed up the way we had just descended. That part of the trail is not one usually sought out by local hikers. The trio's spotless daypacks, sturdy boots, and business-like demeanor made them seem somehow different than most of the folks out for a day on our trails. And it was getting late in the day for a start up that route. That and the fact that each carried a slung rifle not heavy enough for any bear that might be encountered, but which would certainly do damage to a hooter in season. Also, the trio passed us without the usual stop to greet, ask about the trail, and talk the way local hikers usually do.

We got back to the trailhead about four o'clock. Dave headed straight for the cooler in his Bronco and got us some brews that had been waiting to quell our thirst before we left for our homes. We chatted for a few minutes about how tough trail upkeep might be even if the huts were made presentable. Windows might help. Then, as I headed out of the parking area, I noticed one vehicle still there. It was a late model Ford van with no side windows and a short antenna clipped onto the driver's side window. For some reason, an errant TV melodrama thought came to mind about whether my car was now bugged.

I got back to my thirty-six foot Tollycraft houseboat home down at the harbor about 5:30. It's an aging fiberglass boat with good lines except for the square topside living area that makes it difficult to handle in any breeze. A long summer evening lay ahead of me with no plans, romantic or otherwise, except to enjoy dinner and what promised to be the usual spectacular Juneau sunset. Maybe it would be an opportunity to catch up reading some of the books and magazines that kept the boat low in the water. Before that came the usual weekend housekeeping chores. This was mainly done by moving enough magazines and mail off the table so that what would pass for dinner could have space on the table. I had a passing thought about doing the week's dishes before I suddenly remembered the package in my pack. As I went forward to get it, the wake from a passing boat rocked my boat. I went to the wheelhouse door to see if one of my neighbors was returning from a day of fishing. Help might be needed catching a line as the tide was ebbing quickly and the winds were rising. We have quirky tide and wind conditions that can make it tough for even the best skipper to dock at times. I saw a forty-footer passing my boat's stern, a trunk cabin model named 'Relentless' with a homeport of Neskowin, Oregon lettered on the stern. The well-polished boat looked custom-built and sounded like it was powered by twin diesels.

The boat was crewed by three guys in spotless white T-shirts, khaki shorts, and tennis shoes. The one at the wheel was operating from the fly bridge and the other two were ready to handle the mooring lines. Somehow their neat clothes reminded me of the hikers we had encountered earlier when we were coming down the trail. The boat docked down at the transient moorage on the main float and tied up. The trio entered the cabin and seemed to be in for the night. I closed my door, pulled the curtains, and went back to the cabin area.

After clearing the dining booth table in the galley by pushing more stuff aside, I put the journal on the table and used a sash brush to clean some of the dirt and mold off the leather cover on to my table and floor. When I tried to work the zipper that held the two sides together it came off in my hands as I pulled. I then folded the leather cover back and found that the ring binder pages inside, while slightly damp and just starting to fade, were still readable. What follows is from the journal and from what I learned about the hunted and the hunters. The questions raised are still lingering around us.

THE JOURNAL STARTED:

"To Chris, Jerry, and Kevin"

Just in case something further happens to us, Mom and I are hoping that someday this journal will be found by someone not chasing us so that you may perhaps find out what happened on our trip, why we have not been more able to keep in touch with you, and above all to let you know that whatever happens, we love you. We pray that if this nightmare ever ends one way or another, we can all be together again. Love Always, Mom and Dad.

The faded writing continued:

Where are we? Who are we now? Are we where we fled to or have we moved on to a perhaps safer place? We can't really tell you because if this journal is found, it might somehow place you in more danger. It's better if we just tell you what happened so that you will know the real story. You do know that it all started the summer that we took our dream trip to California as we finally were coming closer to being bona fide empty nesters. With two of you headed back to college and one off in the service, we were ready to enjoy being just the two of us until grandkids came on the scene. After the precious years of raising you guys, it was a chance for us to have some time together while you were able to enjoy a summer without us to remind you to drive carefully, and to wear your life jackets or bike helmets all the time. We were looking forward to some unplanned time together.

Our trip was to be around thirty days in the San Diego area, maybe a few days of that over in the desert in East San Diego County, maybe some jaunts south of the border into Mexico. We had no firm timetable, just wander and enjoy. Maybe I would join Mom in touring a few antique stores along with doing lots of beach walking. Maybe I would even try some deep sea fishing on a half-day boat out of Point Loma. We planned to take time to check out the Seaport Village scene, which wasn't there when I did my navy time around San Diego. And, yes kids, a few romantic moonlit walks on the beach after a leisurely dinner at one of the places out on Shelter Island. So off we headed trying not to worry - and ended up causing everyone else to worry.

After a day of flying west and south with a long delay at the Los Angeles Airport - how many TV lounges can one airport have? - we landed in San Diego late in the afternoon. Landing at the San Diego Airport was the same thrill as ever, what with the touchdown being so close to the main streets. As we walked off the plane, the terminal seemed to be filled with suntanned people in shorts, sandals, and colorful shirts or halters. There was almost a Margaritaville electricity in the air among the people arriving to enjoy the San Diego scene and those who had been part of it but now had to return to their routines. Suddenly we made a quantum change from being 'on the way' to being in a holiday mood. Everything around us seemed so bright and tropical, busy yet with an atmosphere of sun, sand, and sea.

We claimed our bags, walked out to the crowded street in front of the terminal and caught the shuttle to the car rental place. We planned to pick up a Buick sedan as I enjoy driving something like that when I travel. The one that the lot guy brought us was a maroon four-door with all the extras that gave a touch of luxury compared to our van. I signed the 'till death do us part' rental agreement, loaded the car with our bags, and we headed up Pacific Highway to the motel on Taylor Street near Old Town. The place dates back to the days when defense contracts were bringing needed revenue to San Diego as the airplane making business was headed elsewhere. It's located where you can get to Mission Valley, downtown, Hillcrest or the beaches quickly, yet feel away from a lot of the city hustle and bustle. Our room was just upstairs from the pool and was neat and clean without frills. The almost reasonable rate was reflected in the see-through towels and washcloths in the bathroom. Except for a brief trip out for a late dinner and a walk on the pier out at Ocean Beach, we were in our room quite early for vacation time. Several weeks of carefree wandering was our only plan.

Our world started to change, though of course we did not know it, as we left for breakfast the next morning. The front desk lady had told us how to get to a bakery and café place up in the Hillcrest area where the locals gathered at sidewalk tables to enjoy breakfast in the sun at a slower pace than is found in the tourist areas. As we started out, your mom, tidy as ever, put the rental car contract in the glove compartment of the car and saw a roll of film in a plastic canister. We left it there intending to call the car rental people later to report it in case some other tourists were looking for it to be able to see their trip highlights. We forgot to make the call about the roll of film, but later decided to turn it in when returning the car at the end of our stay.

What I didn't know then was how many people who had not rented this car were looking for the same roll of film and why.

What we did do, however, was to pass the days being carefree tourists taking zoo pictures, Old Town pictures, lighthouse pictures, anything of remote interest pictures that could be gone over later. When we were not out enjoying San Diego, we were inside our private world having a second honeymoon. Our often-hummed theme song seemed to be a few bars from "Something that happened for the first time seems to be happening again." Then one afternoon we finally dropped off our rolls of film at a one-hour photo place in a shopping area off Midway Drive not far from the motel. I chatted with the suntanned girl behind the counter for a minute and realized she was someone you guys would have liked to meet. The left -behind canister was now in my stuff back at the motel rather than in the hot car.

On our way to dinner that evening, we swung by the photo place to get our prints just before the shop closed. As I parked in front of the building and got out, two large men in baggy shorts and loud Hawaiian shirts hurried from the shop. One of them walked with a rolling gait as if he had a bad knee. Something about the way he walked was elusively familiar. He glanced toward me with a sort of 'don't I know you from somewhere' glance as they quickly entered a waiting car with a third man at the wheel and left.

Mom had stayed in the car as I entered the shop. I remember her telling me to be sure I got double prints so that we could send a set back to you. Those are the last words I remember from before. Then as I went from the bright evening sun of the parking lot into the shop, my eyes suddenly adjusted to a scene of horror. The cash register was on the floor and the place was completely trashed. Strips of developed negatives were strewn everywhere. Envelopes of prints waiting for pickup were scattered on the floor behind the counter. The pretty dark-haired clerk I had joked with earlier was lying doubled up in death behind the counter showing how much violence had been done to her during the ransacking of the shop. I moved a heavy tripod that lay across her body as I confirmed that she was really dead. Then, not knowing how to react, wondering if the guys who had driven away would return, I backed out the door almost knocking over another customer entering the shop.

Somehow I got back to the car and into the driver's seat. I fumbled the key into the ignition and, ignoring Mom's questions, jammed the car into gear. I managed to avoid a gray carryall parked near us and accelerated out of the parking lot and away from the scene that had just been burned into my mind. As I turned right onto Midway, a police car with no sirens or lights operating turned past us into the parking area and headed for the area of the photo shop.

By then, Mom was really wondering what was going on. "What's the hurry? Are you all right? Weren't the pictures ready?" were her first questions. Others followed as I did not answer, trying only to drive, to distance myself from what I had just seen. Still in shock, I kept going on driving automatically through the lights at Rosecrans and finally managed to pull into another strip mall parking lot. I was able to stop the car and get my head out the door before depositing my stomach contents onto the pavement. None of the people in the cars passing by seemed to think that was the least bit unusual.

After that I was able to tell her about the dead clerk and the trashed shop. At least she did not chide me for not staying in the store until the police arrived. We left the car where it was and walked to a burger place near the street at the end of the shopping strip. I cleaned up a bit in the men's room and joined her at a table. As we had a cold drink and talked about what to do next, she suggested that I look to where our parked rental car was now surrounded by a team of police officers with guns drawn as a tow truck arrived to haul it away. In the midst of the scene I had a fleeting thought that public barfing must be a serious crime in these parts. Then I saw someone from one of the stores talking to an officer and pointing toward the burger place. I vaguely wondered why the officer would be thinking about food at a time like this. More police cars were arriving along with a canine unit.

Also arriving along Rosecrans was a city bus which came to a stop just outside the burger place. We managed to get outside and board the bus before the search teams headed our way. At least your mother managed not to panic, saying only, "Twenty some years ago you promised me an exotic vacation sometime but not like this."

My thoughts were more on what to do next -

make my non-involvement known to the police or keep moving. After all, what had I done to be concerned about? Or was I - or we - now a target for a killer? Then I realized that the bus had passed our motel. Seeing no sign that the rental car papers had led the police there yet, we got off at the next stop stepping into a crowd of tourists. As we walked back to our room, I saw a gray carryall in frantic pursuit of the bus we had been on.

When we entered the welcome shelter of our room, I turned the TV on to see if there was any news about the events. There it was: a news helicopter was hovering overhead as it filmed the murder scene below. Than a shot of the rental car being towed. Rushed reporter words luridly talked about a couple that had fled the scene and were suspected of possible involvement in the murder. I could see what looked like the gray carryall that I had almost hit parked some distance away from the police activity. There was even a distant view of us boarding the city bus. I wondered if the desk clerk in the motel lobby was watching the news and matching the pieces to fit us and our car.

After quickly changing clothes, we shoved as much stuff as possible into the daypacks we had brought to use on our backcountry walks. The rest of our luggage and a few items in the rental car would probably be history. We left the keys in the room and quickly left the motel. At least we could try to blend in with the other thousands of visitors roaming the city. We headed across the street toward the Old Town area where eager hoards of souvenir-seeking tourists roamed in search of the ultimate gift for Aunt Bertie back home in Iowa. Mingling with the crowds, we tried to appear as casual as they seemed to be. Chances were that most of them were not the subject of a police search.

Somewhere during our strolling we came to a curbside area where shuttle vans from area hotels and resorts parked as they carried guests back and forth.   We boarded one headed back to Mission Valley and got off at a hotel there. From there it was easy enough to stand in front for a while then board the motel's airport shuttle van.   One-step further away from confrontation. We used the same routine to get from the airport to a hotel near downtown. From there it was a short walk to the trolley system and a ride toward the international border. We were last witnessed by riders we talked with as we headed toward the official crossing. We then shop stalled before reversing direction and heading back toward the city. The trolley let us off near the waterfront.

What we needed to do now was to get out of the area as soon as possible. The murder seemed to be local or area news so distance would be helpful. We would also need someone to find out more about what had happened and to keep us informed of what was going on. As we talked, Mom, always thinking, asked if we needed an attorney and I agreed that was maybe a good idea. So far, she had accepted the moving around without objection but now was starting to wonder whether we had made the right choice.

That was when I remembered Ernie.   I had promised to call him while we were in town but so far had been enjoying not having any time committed for social things even with an old friend. I knew him from my prior days in San Diego before I left my navy role; there to return to school and my Midwestern roots with eventual domestication by your mother. It was a sort of reversal from the usual role of heading west to seek the Southern California lifestyle.

My old navy friend now practiced law when and where he chose to rather than enjoying the comfort and prestige of his family firm long established in the city power structure. Perhaps he was too much of a maverick to fit that mold. We had kept in touch over the years when either of us happened to travel to the other's area. And, as our friendship had started during my navy time, he happened to be my oldest known friend.

When I managed to reach him at his home number, his first comment was, "Are you the tourists that folks seem to be looking for?" My stunned silence apparently answered his question.

Then he proceeded to tell me a few 'new' lame attorney jokes. As I became calmer, he switched to the role of attorney helping a new client. He said, "Take a stroll on the sidewalk north of the restaurant called 'Star of The Sea' and the old sailing ship tied up near it. Snap a few tourist pictures of each other. Keep an eye out for a green Chevy Blazer with a bike rack on top. See you in fifteen or twenty minutes."

Which is how we, the hunted, came to spend the first night of our new journey in a guesthouse overlooking the ocean near San Diego. After being whisked off the city waterfront and out to the beach area, we talked with our host and now legal adviser over a late dinner and glasses of good wine. He suggested that most likely no legal charges had yet been filed though we were probably being sought for questioning and did have some options. For the present, why not continue our vacation? But, for reasons he would explain, no calls home except for one he would make from a pay phone to tell the kids not to worry too much just because their folks had dropped out of sight. And don't use your credit cards.

When we expressed total ignorance about why or how we, the most innocent of tourists, were ipso facto fugitives, he took a deep breath and said that it could be related to some local rumors and happenings. It was mostly stuff that he had picked up on around town and at the courthouse as he made his daily rounds in and out of various courtrooms and offices.

He reminded us that a major national political party had held a nomination convention in San Diego just before we arrived. All had gone according to plan as the incumbent was presented, accepted and accoladed for another term. Sometime after the acceptance speech and before the standard bearer left town, something unknown had happened. No one was talking specifics enough to print anything or speak about it in detail. A lid was on and controls were in place against leaks. Someone, perhaps a tourist, perhaps a reporter or photographer for one of the screaming tabloids had gotten into the right - or wrong room - or had a photo op vantage point and apparently taken some most interesting pictures.

As Ernie talked, he paced back and forth in the den as though addressing a jury. His tall frame and suntanned face supported a last ring of graying hair. We could imagine how he must appear in court; dignified, even courtly with an aura of sincerity and conviction. I tried to remember how he looked when I first arrived in San Diego as an eighteen-year-old navy recruit when he was the officer detailed to meet me at the airport.

He continued, "Then a photographer known to freelance and sell his stuff to the highest bidder but currently working as a maintenance man at a local hotel was killed under somewhat unusual circumstances in a bathroom at the airport after parking a rental car near the terminal. No film was found in his camera or on the body or in the luggage in his hotel room. His rental car had been picked up by the efficient company so that it could quickly be rented again. Could we have found some film?"

We didn't answer.

He paused, reflected for a moment, and commented, "The death of the clerk doesn't seem to fit something any federal agency would do so openly. Perhaps some other less image conscious group was also after the film."

He switched back to his prior track. "These are just bits and pieces that could add up to something or could be absolutely nothing. Let me put the known 'facts' on the table. We know that the convention happened as scheduled and as planned. Now it's off to the campaign trail with no known roadblocks. No DWIs as far as anyone knows, no undisclosed mental health history, no recent real estate deals that left investors wondering who had done what to whom. The show leaves town except for part of the security detail. Some of their vans are still taking up space at the Federal Building. Then, not related in any known way, is the death of a tabloid photo taker out at the airport, and a death by tripod of a photo shop clerk. Those two deaths might be related. Then we also have the death of a cross-dresser near downtown with a copy of a release from a federal lockup stuffed into his bra.

Which, if all this is related, could make interesting copy for the San Diego Union."

When he said this, Mom gulped audibly. Ernie looked at her and said, "Do you by any chance have a roll of film that you didn't take?"

Which we did. Then he added, "Maybe I would prefer not to have an answer to that."

So our choices seemed to be to go to the police and trust them with the film or to call the Secret Service and work with them. The Secret Service probably would not even admit that the film existed or that anything was going on. Either way whoever else was involved in any of the events would not know who had the film and we had no way to get in touch with them. And we would still be in danger.

Ernie summed it up by saying, "You're right. And if you were able to give them any film that you might have, they win, you lose, the country could lose. It would certainly be a field day for the tabloid business and the other political party. It might be time to drop out until any danger passes, maybe extend your dream vacation a bit."

"So where could we go while all this is happening?," Mom asked. "Can we really hide somewhere, anywhere?"

At that time I mentioned Alaska as being a faraway place off most beaten tracks. Several years earlier while scanning an outdated magazine during the usual wait to be seen by a doctor, I read an article telling about a novel use of some extremely large culvert pipe. I had been intrigued by the way the pipes became crew shelters on a rugged power line project in Alaska, a place I had always wanted to see. If the danger to us was great, why not 'go to ground' in a place like that.

At least it seemed remote enough and far away enough to be worth checking out or even becoming part of.

At this point the reality of our situation and the thought of being 'on the run' caused Mom to go into a near meltdown. She had been under obvious stress during the events of the past few hours yet taking the series of events in stride. Now the total impact of going from carefree vacationer to semi-fugitive seemed to sink in more fully.

"What about the kids? What about the house? What about everything?," she blurted as the tears started to flow and the meltdown became total.

I took her hand as I said to Ernie, "We need to talk."

We walked outside to where a deck overlooked the ocean. The tears kept coming as I held her. That and the distant sound of the surf seemed to calm her a bit, yet the thought of dropping out from all that was so normal for even a short time was overwhelming her. Not wanting to load more on her but realizing that she needed to know why my choice was to run, I told her my reason.

Afterwards, she walked to the deck rail and stood in silence looking toward the water. I felt helpless, not able to reach where she was, yet knowing that whatever happened next, our relationship was changed in ways that we could not completely understand for a long time, if ever.

Finally, she turned to me and said, "We met when you were 24. We have been married for 22 years and have always shared in every way. I have to accept that you had good reasons for not telling me earlier what you just told me. It's obviously going to take me some time to work through this but, for now, we, emphasis on we, go."

We returned inside to where Ernie was waiting. Mom asked, "How do we become dropouts?"

That night in the guesthouse, after plans were made, we held each other tightly as we listened to the surf pounding and the night sounds outside.

FIRST THINGS FIRST

We did finally manage to sleep soundly for a few hours before waking to the sounds of surf and seagulls outside the sunlit bedroom. Mom looked over at me and wondered if all the previous afternoon and evening had perhaps been a chocolate-inspired dream. I assured her that I wished it had been rather than being reality. Reluctantly we emerged into the new day and new life. We showered, dressed, and headed for the kitchen.

Our host and his wife greeted us with coffee and the promise of a breakfast that would fuel us for the first part of our journey. Apparently they had been married long enough that she did not inquire about our circumstances though the front page of the morning paper gave strong hints of who we might be. As we finished eating, she excused herself and went off to take a walk on the beach with the family dogs.

Having made our choice, our immediate need was to do some basic chores to get our new life underway. Some of it you already know about. The letter we wrote, without specific details of why, was a joint effort of Mom and me. It lacked more details of the events leading up to our plight because the less you knew, the less you could tell and maybe be less dangerous to us or to 'them', whoever they were.

Because we had no idea how long our absence would be, we just had to fly-by-wire and leave it up to you guys to do your best. We had total faith that you would. We also asked that you not tell anyone who we might have called in San Diego - and to burn the letter or lock it up in the box at the bank. As far as the practical part, it gave you information for access to the money market account at the bank so that money could be transferred for bill paying and school expenses. We included a general power of attorney in case you needed to do any paper signing. We arranged for it to be mailed from the main post office after we left.

I hope that you were able to convince the neighbors and others such as our church friends that we had just decided to take a one-year sabbatical of sorts to travel, work, and volunteer blaming it on the mid-life exposure to a different place.

THE ROAD NORTH

After breakfast, we huddled with Ernie in his den to further plan our journey into limbo. Even the leisurely breakfast on the deck had done little to cushion the concerns we had. Yet the rabid TV news about the ongoing search motivated us even more to move on. The morning was spent on thinking about the mundane details of disappearing along with backup plans to cover what might happen along the way. Mom focused on the details; perhaps it was her way to not be totally overwhelmed by what we were heading toward or away from. Ernie insisted on ways for us to keep in touch that would assure him of our safety while outlining what he would do if we didn't check in. We agreed to read the legal notices in any place we landed. If we saw one seeking heirs of a Rankin J. Pilford, we would contact him. It seemed very cloak and daggerish to all of us but necessary.

By noon we found ourselves headed through Ocean Beach toward where I-10 ends or starts. Then we headed north on I-5 in the Blazer up the hill past the La Jolla turnoff. We carried identifications loaned by attorney and spouse along with borrowed credit cards and cash. A ski boat loaded with coolers and water toys being towed behind us provided further cover. If we drove steadily north for between thirty and forty hours of road time, we would be near Seattle and could take time to rest.

We rolled along through the beach communities and miles of tracts on the San Diego-Los Angeles corridor that seemed to include all the pastel colored condos ever built. The Border Patrol checkpoint up near Oceanside had been one of our concerns, but we were waived on through after quickly answering the questions about citizenship and place of birth. But did I perhaps notice two of those gray carryall type vehicles similar to the one that had hung back from the search scene in San Diego? Or was I starting to be paranoid about a fairly commonplace vehicle?

About two hours later we were on our way past Disneyland without even stopping to see Mickey and Minnie. A detour was made to drop off the boat and trailer in one of the ubiquitous southwest Los Angeles suburbs at a boat repair shop parking lot for a later pickup as planned by our attorney. We gradually crept back toward I-5 and continued north through the local insanity called normal freeway traffic fearing more from the other drivers than from our hunters. Every Mercedes, Jaguar, and BMW ever built seemed to be rolling along beside us. The journey was a litany of creep, speed, and stop and repeat the cycle. Though our trip was only three hours old, we were already feeling quite intimate with the Blazers seats as we endured the fumes, noise, and monotony.

A long hour was spent in getting to the east-west, north-south I-5, I-10 interchange near the heart of downtown LA. We spun like clothes in a drier through the multi-levels of off and on ramps and finally were able to exit to I-5 north. After collective sighs of relief at being out of that particular maelstrom, another hour brought us to the lower parts of what the Golden Staters call the

Grapevine that you go up and over to reach the heat of the Central Valley. First you drive up and up an hour or more on three or more lanes watching three or more lanes cavorting downhill. Mom and I were in a state of awe at the spectacle of dry brush, green hills in the distance, and so many cars, semi-trucks, RVs, and pickups of every description playing games of bumper tag with no apparent concern for safe driving. We finally reached the summit near Gorman and pulled off into a rest area for a stretch and driver change.

Then we headed north again down into the heat of the Central Valley. The bigger trucks are limited to thirty miles an hour at places along this stretch and have special lanes to use if their brakes fail. Mom commented again about the difference between this and the mostly flat country back home. "Wish we were there, not here," I commented. Finally the pavement started to level out as we approached the valley floor.

Cotton fields (not back home), oil pumping rigs, lots of growing stuff and even cows started to border the freeway. Hot seemed to be the only way to describe it. We had made a pit stop for gas and Big Macs before seeing this stretch of scenery. No signs of pursuit at the burger counter but heads up as we returned to the car, air conditioned it back to comfort, placed soft drinks in the cup holders, and were, as Willie would sing, on the road again.

Around Bakersfield, we checked the map and opted to take Old 99 North through the Central Valley rather than be penned in on the faster I-5 freeway route that parallels the California Aqueduct, which takes precious Northern California water to the thirsty folks in Los Angeles for watering lawns and washing cars with. There would be more exit options on the old route if we needed them with towns to drive through along the way. We took turns at the wheel with only the non-driver allowed to nap. There wasn't any discussion of our reasons for running. Each of us stored our thoughts; perhaps it was TMI, too much information, for now.

Another pit stop was made near Fresno, then on toward Sacramento. Nothing was said on the hourly news on the radio about two people headed north away from the law, not even a mention of the San Diego murder. Life in the Central Valley seemed to revolve around crop reports and western music. Then signs announced that Manteca (is that grease in Spanish?) was the next town. About that time, Mom commented about the crop dusting planes we had seen over the fields near the highway. Very skillful flying under the power lines, turn quickly and back down the field - but don't they spray something? We recalled the movie "North By Northwest," that long-ago Cary Grant epic, pondered, and kept going.

Then we saw the same act somewhere between Lodi and Sacramento. I pulled the Blazer off the highway at the next service area, got out and opened the tailgate, bent over to pick up deliberately dropped keys, and saw a small black box stuck under the back bumper. It came off easily and, as we had no use for it, I left it in a similar spot on a county sheriff's car parked in front of a café. The find confirmed our fears that someone wanted to find us or at least know where we were or which way we were headed. I hoped that they were the guys wearing the white hats.

Though the miles of sitting were getting to both of us, we moved on through the traffic and sprawl of Sacramento without stopping. Then we crossed off Roseville, Lincoln, Marysville, Chico, Mt. Shasta and a lot of other places we had never known existed till then. We finally made it out of California with no stops except for gas, fast food, and to drain and change drivers. It was no time to enjoy the scenery, just put on miles to separate us from anyone looking for us regardless of seat ache and a desire to change clothes.

We didn't do a lot of talking about our plight till sometime after Red Bluff and Redding not long before we came to the lower side of Oregon. Mom woke up and got a notebook from her purse. It's one that she uses to sketch ideas of things she wants me to build around the house or to jot down sayings that she hears that she wants to remember. She started to write as I drove on. After about twenty miles of silence, she started to read to me what she had written:

1. I found some film in a car that you rented.

2. You saw a very dead person in a photo shop.

3. You almost backed into a carryall that showed up at our next stop.

4. The local police were arriving as we left the photo shop.

5. Something happened that apparently involved the president.

6. The San Diego police would like to talk to you.

7. The film may be wanted by the Secret Service and the people who had it taken.

8. If we step forward, your history may come to light.

Therefore, various people want to talk to us or to dispose of us but we have leverage in control of the film and until any chaser knows for sure that our demise will/won't expose the president, maybe the intent will be to not make a direct move but to find, follow and even scare us. With that, she torn the sheet of paper into small pieces, rolled the window down, violated the California litter law by tossing the pieces out, and went back to sleep. I drove on.

Ten hours of Oregon and Washington was the last long push before Seattle announced its' nearness with more monster traffic and truck-enhanced rough pavement for the two weary road veterans to deal with. By that time we were beyond highway hypnosis and counting down every mile left to go. Thirty-plus hours of road time had finally brought us from a police search in San Diego to Seattle and possible breathing room for now.

At last we were able to follow the signs to SEATAC, the local airport. The long-term parking lot was zeroed in on and the Blazer parked and locked for Ernie to have picked up later. As we got out, there was the distinct impression that the back of our clothes now matched the seat cushions. The parking lot shuttle bus got us to the main terminal and we didn't have to drive. A time-out was jointly declared to wash up a bit, put on something fresh from our backpacks, get a shave for me, and allow Mom to shop for her needs. The various gift shops provided some local tourist items such as sweatshirts and hats. Now where could we rest and plan our next move?

A walk to the baggage claim area led to a rack of ads and phones where we tried to decide which one might be not cheap but not main line. Our choice was one called The Shadows. Press a phone button and a shuttle was on the way. It turned out to be less than ten minutes away in the shadow of a big chain operation. Maybe it caught their overflow or provided a haven for travelers and others making brief layovers. There was a 24-hour dining spot next to both places where we ate before crashing. We took turns sleeping fitfully over the next twelve hours. At least the bed wasn't headed down a highway.

As the sounds of jets departing from SEATAC awoke us, we made insipid motel coffee and thought about how to get further north without being in a car. Flying would be quick and easy but seemed too obvious. Going somewhere by boat seemed possible but isn't a passport needed to enter most other countries? Even Canada would want some sort of proper identification. Were we willing to risk trying to use our borrowed drivers licenses? Was there an APB that might show up at a border crossing? So I called the recorded information number for the Alaska Marine Highway System and found that the Columbia was scheduled to leave on its northbound run in about six hours. There was room for walk-ons and perhaps even a cabin.

We walked over to the chain restaurant for a quick breakfast, took the motel shuttle back to the airport, and found an express bus to take us down to the heart of Seattle. Some new clothes and bigger backpacks seemed in order to replace our California gear. A cab took us to REI where we made the switch from a chino-clad guy with wife in sun and sand outfit to jeans-clad couple wearing hiking boots and vests on their way to Alaska. A cab took us to the pier where cars were already starting to load onto the ship. We even managed to get a cabin due to a cancellation. Then we boarded the Columbia for the fifty-four hour run to Alaska.

While we waited for the last of the loading and boarding, a tour of our temporary home seemed in order. The main deck had a covered solarium area forward on the bow where passengers were already setting up camp in tents and on air mattresses. It was starting to look like a public campground on a holiday weekend complete with music provided by the campers. For those not wanting to camp on a steel deck, there was lounge area with chairs that could be slept in. Food was available at a snack bar or in a more formal dining room. Our choice was to take things from the snack bar to our cabin and stay away from the crowded solarium and lounge.

As the car deck door finally swung closed, the gangplank was lifted, and lines cast off, the moment seemed to be somehow symbolic of how our lives had been rapidly changed. With that sobering thought, we left the rail for a further tour of the ship and, specifically, the car deck. No official-looking gray carryalls were to be seen among the cars, trucks and RVs packed into the vast area where passengers with pets would be down later for pet potty time. As the sun set, we stood at the rail watching while the ship headed toward the Inside Passage. At each port of call - Ketchikan, Wrangell and Petersburg - we discretely watched comings and goings, foot and car, for anything unusual. When we ventured from our cabin to eat or walk for exercise, our fellow passengers seemed to be a blend of tourists, Alaskans returning home, and others such as Coast Guard personnel headed for duty in Juneau.

The Columbia arrived at Auke Bay near Juneau at 11:30 in the evening, past sunset even at the time of the year when we first saw Alaska. A heavy rain was falling which seemed to be expected. Lines were tossed, caught, and secured to the dock as the ship maneuvered back and forth to tie up. After watching the docking from the main deck to see if anyone or anything stood out, we descended to the car deck and hung back in the line of passengers walking up the ramp from the car deck to a parking lot where cars and people were waiting to board. Baggage carts hustled back and forth loading and unloading luggage and ship supplies. We didn't see anyone looking like the law checking out the arriving passengers. Looking for a way to get to downtown Juneau about 14 miles away, we passed a line of cabs and boarded a blue bus with a sign saying "Ptarmigan Transport - $5.00 to town." It seemed like the quickest way to town.

The driver greeted us like we were old friends returning to town. He had a full beard and was clad in flannel shirt, bright suspenders holding up high mileage jeans, and rubber boots. His rain gear was hanging over the driver's seat drying out. He apparently knew some of the other passengers as he talked fishing to them when they boarded. We began to sense that Juneau might be a friendly place that strangers could meld into quite easily.

A seat at the rear of the bus seemed a good place to listen to the rain beating on the roof and to try to see the road as the bus lumbered out of the parking area. No houses were visible and only a few lights pierced the rain until a closed gas station and a post office sign told us we were in and out of Auke Bay. Minutes later more lights and traffic signals appeared as the Mendenhall Valley came and went. Lights blazing over an empty Fred Meyer Store parking lot briefly glowed through the rain. Then there seemed to be a lake to the left and a channel to the right. A few miles later more signs of civilization started to appear through the downpour: more water on our right, a lighted motel sign saying "The Breakwater" barely visible to our left, a lighted bridge to somewhere on the right, another motel sign to the left with a faint image of a prospector, then we were, apparently, 'Downtown.'

The bus turned left away from the water and up a narrow and steep one-way street through what appeared to be the business area. We got off at the Baranoff which seemed to be the big hotel in the middle of everything that was not happening at that time of night. I found an open cabstand nearby that smelled of stale beer and stored cigarette butts. A well-aged Chevy sedan driven by a guy with jeans, rubber boots, and a flannel shirt was called to take us to the Breakwater. We were beginning to get an idea of how people dressed in Juneau. The cab ride to the motel was fast even though the cab seemed ready for retirement. The motel overlooked the four-lane main road into town and the harbor and was within walking distance of downtown. We used our loaned names and a made-up address, paid cash for a three-night stay, and tried to sleep. Welcome to Alaska. The rain continued.

That is how we got up here where we thought that the heat was off. As our stay lengthened, that turned out to be a major misconception.

OUR TOWN - SETTLING IN

I awoke to the background murmur of traffic noise somewhere outside of our room. Still somewhat groggy from the long drive, the ferry trip, and the late check-in, I put on coffee in the motel mini-pot and headed for the shower. When I came out, Mom was awake but still under the covers. "Was that a cab or a stock car racer that brought us here? And do I really remember seeing the pavement through the floorboards?", were her only comments.

I brought her a cup of coffee which she carried as she disappeared into the bathroom. While she prepared for our first day here, I opened the curtains and saw that the traffic noise was from a flood of inbound cars on the road toward downtown. Across the four-lane road was a boat harbor. It was small by San Diego standards but huge by mid-west comparisons. Across the channel was an island with snow-capped mountains topping it. I could see homes along a road on the island. The rain had stopped, at least for a while and the sun was up. Floatplanes seemed to be heading toward landing in the harbor past a distant bridge. I didn't see any gray vans or a SWAT team so perhaps we were safe for a while.

After we cautiously emerged from the shelter of our room in search of food, we found the motel dining room and were seated at a table overlooking the harbor. Mom was pleasantly surprised by the surroundings. "Cloth napkins, a tablecloth, all the nice things," she softly commented, "Are we really in Alaska? It's not the way I imagined it would be. No bears and no igloos. It seems like a really nice place."

I explained to her that it was, contrary to what many tourists thought, an actual state of the union, used the same currency, and spoke the same language though there were Native and Indian cultures that carried on their traditions. That much I had learned as we were headed north. With that we started to talk about what we would do next. There was a need to somehow let Ernie know our status without leaving any trace of where we were. Then there was a need for some decisions to be made about our immediate plans. At least we probably had a few days or weeks head start on any followers.

With that thought, we decided to take a walk, stretch our muscles a bit, and see what was around us. We headed out of the motel with a sketchy walking tour map from a lobby stand and walked along Glacier Avenue toward town. After passing the high school, a swimming pool, the Marine Highway Headquarters, and a grade school appropriately named Harborview, we stopped to look at the map. Lesson One in how to look new in town. We decided to turn left and head toward the mountain that seemed to loom over the city. That took us to a large green area that turned out to be the place where the city founders are buried. Wandering through the residential area high on the hill led us to a wooden flume where water from a creek was being channeled down toward the city. The flume was covered and had planks for walking on it so we kept going. When it ended near a gravel road, we looked at our map and guessed that we were on something called Basin Road near a wooden bridge over the creek.

Civilization seemed to be to the right down the road. Soon there were houses that seemed to defy gravity and common sense as they clung out in space over the steep slope. Those on the uphill side didn't have much space for on-street parking or front porches or for the tour buses that competed with cars using the road. At Seventh Street, which seemed to be the last street up from the water we turned right and ended up at the top of Main Street. The walk down toward the capitol building demonstrated how downhill walking can be harder than uphill so we took the stairs there down to another street and headed back to our room. Being out in the fresh air exercising and enjoying scenery like we had never seen before had raised our lagging spirits greatly. Along the way we had a late lunch at a great place called The Fiddlehead after a local fern. As we enjoyed the meal, I heard your mother say, "If we have to hide, the food here is even better than San Diego."

She had just discovered a local treat called North Douglas Chocolate Cake. We were both beginning to like the community in spite of why we were here.

Now a few more words about where we were when this was written. Around 28 or 30,000 people live up here in Southeast Alaska in the capital city of Juneau. It's a big city (borough) in area as it covers around 4,200 square miles, but most of the people live in town, not 'out the road.' 'In town' could mean the original town along the channel that the city grew up from, or might include the West Juneau/Douglas area across the bridge or, to those further out the road, might include the more recently settled 'Valley' seven miles from downtown. It can be confusing because if you are in the Valley, you can go further 'out the road' but if you are in town, heading 'out the road' might mean just going out to the Valley area. A person downtown would probably just say 'going to the Valley' to avoid confusion. The Valley is more like the housing tracts with malls that you grew up knowing. At least wherever you go up here there are mountains to look at - if you can see them through the rain.

The downtown area is like a small San Francisco with steep streets heading up from the harbor along Gastineau Channel to the houses overlooking the state capital and the downtown business area. It has a sense of history coming from both the native culture and the mining era. Now it is a place where tides of tourists ebb and flow from April to late September or early October every year as the cruise ships come and go and Alaska Airlines arrives with more visitors. They buy T-shirts, visit the Red Dog Saloon, perhaps take a bus tour out to the Mendenhall Glacier or visit the salmon bake for a 'real' Alaska experience. Many also tour the Alaska State Museum and the smaller mining museum. Some even manage to hike the area trails though most don't want to venture too far from the pre-paid meals on the cruise ships. What they mainly see, however, is Front Street which runs along what used to be the channel from Main to Franklin. Main heads up past the state capitol and parallels Seward and Franklin. These streets form much of the downtown business area. Franklin becomes South Franklin where cruise ships dock and tour buses load up. It is a very compact downtown that served a smaller city well in the past. Now much of the retail business for groceries and clothes has moved to the Valley. It's still possible, though, to see a doctor or dentist, go to a church or a movie, or enjoy a good meal downtown. From town or valley you can, within minutes, hike, fish, or ski. The hard part is deciding where and what from all the choices.

What they don't see to any extent is how much all this history is surrounded by water and forests and glaciers with a lot of very rugged terrain to enjoy. Before the recent cheechakos arrived to become Alaskans, there were the gold seekers and before them the natives that lived off the land and water. They are still around us trying to keep their rich heritage alive. It is a lovely scenic place. Aside from the scenery, the thing we notice the most is the people and their sense of community. It's a place where you can fit in easily, and see people you know on the streets or in the stores.

We decided to become immersed in the community right away which helped to give us needed protective coloration. As we settled in to our new life, we were accepted without questions as to what we did for a living or where we came from. Of course as we shopped at the Foodland grocery store downtown there was some sticker shock which did take some time to adjust to. Food items and everything else gets here by water or air which adds to the cost. But enough of the tour guide role and on to our life here.

During out first days here we spent a lot of time walking around the downtown area trying to become acquainted with our temporary home. We watched as the masses of state and federal workers arrived by car and bus each weekday morning (except for their very numerous state and federal holidays) to enter the state and federal buildings, emerged at noon to eat, walk and shop, and left around 4:30 for their town and valley homes.

On one of our walks we wandered into a place called Centennial Hall where a lot of local events are held. At the Forest Service Visitor Center there, we looked at the displays that told about the Tongass National Forest, the history, and the outdoor recreation available all around us. As we picked up copies of the local trail guides, it was easy to decide how we would spend our summer while watching for whomever might be hunting for us as we planned our next move. That would also offer a chance to check out the abandoned shelters.

After our ride on the blue bus into town, we began thinking and talking about the best way to blend into the community in very subtle ways that would not tag us as new in town. We finally decided that it's mostly about not having been there and then being there at various places without being obvious. You don't go around saying "Hi there, I'm new in town" or making a big show by being overly friendly or pushy. It's more the obvious things like showing up at a church as a new member that could lead to too many coffee time questions.

Conversely, thanking the clerk at the grocery store, asking the butcher for a not too special cut of meat, having the guy at the service station check under the hood gave nodding acquaintances with people we would see again and again. We planned to be seen in the local stores and at the restaurants as just another couple that came and went. And reading the local paper along with books on local and state history would give us background we could use in conversations with folks we encountered along the way.

A place to stay was another concern we faced. Not knowing how long our exile would last - days, months, or even years - confused the issue. Southeast Alaska for various reasons aside from bugs, bears, and weather is not the ideal place to camp out year-round. Campgrounds are few and the Forest Service cabins are not for long term occupancy. Motel and hotel rates are high in the winter and impossible for more than a short stay in the summer. Even Bill Gates brought his own boat one year when he came to Juneau to celebrate a birthday. Seasonal workers do some camping out or share rooms but we were not yet ready for that or sleeping in a car at the Yacht Club parking lot. Buying a house or trying to rent an apartment, though, might get us involved in a credit check that we didn't want to confront.

As we walked around town in those early days here shopping from Foodland to Super Bear, we noticed many bulletin boards which seemed to be the local way of selling cars and boats, job hunting, and announcing local fundraisers. That's how we learned about house sitting. Year round but more so in the winter, local folks like to leave town for long periods to avoid the tourist season or the legislative session or just to see sunshine. Fear of power outages and frozen pipes, a need to walk left-behind dogs, or just to have the lights on make it nice to have someone in the house while gone. Folks who are willing to live a semi-nomadic lifestyle and want to avoid rent or mortgage payments and can accept the challenge of moving every few weeks or months make good house sitters. It seemed like a logical way for us to go considering our uncertain status.

As we were able to present a reasonably acceptable appearance and looked honest enough not to clean out the refrigerator and liquor cabinet, we opted for that route. Our approach was that we were early retirees looking around to find where we wanted to spend our golden years. Having no-cost shelter and the occasional use of a car made the deals even sweeter.

Our first such 'home' was out on what is called Back Loop Road. It's probably called that because it's the back part of Loop Road which circles around the Mendenhall Valley housing suburbia from Mendenhall Boulevard around to where it joins Glacier Highway again just before Auke Bay about ten or eleven miles from downtown.

We were able to sit for two months for a University of Alaska couple at their home near the Juneau campus as they headed 'outside' for the lower forty-eight. The house was a two-story log home well away from the road with a view of Auke Lake and the mountains. It was on the bus line so we could travel into town that way or use an aging Subaru sedan with what is called locally a 'Juneau body' which is a car that runs but leaves clouds of rust. A store called DeHarts that sells basic groceries, snacks, drinks and bait was within walking distance down at the junction.

The house offered privacy and isolation with no really close neighbors so we felt reasonably secure. Two left-behind family dogs helped our comfort level. The couple was sure that two months of retirement in Juneau would show that life in Southeast Alaska would be right for us. The location also allowed us to walk to the Auke Bay Post Office for the occasional general delivery letter that came for us. Another plus factor was that we were close to several major trails that offer a variety of challenges such as

East and West Glacier Trails, Spaulding Meadows, and the Auke Lake Trail. With a roof over our heads for the time being, we started hiking and blending in to the community.

While we were trying to make it through our own life style changes, we were unaware of a very tragic event that had apparently happened several months earlier on a highway in the more remote areas of eastern San Diego County. Most likely we would never have known of it except that it provided the way for us to go even deeper into our new life.

The accident had provided brief grist for the local media evening news at the time but then became only another sad statistic for the record keepers. A couple was driving to San Diego from a mid-sized city in Ohio. They were a baby boomer era couple who had opted out of the 'raise a family' path. Dual careers were followed instead up to the time parents were buried. The career paths had left no time for close friends or community links and no family ties existed any longer, so why not have a garage sale, sell the house, and head west with minimal stuff to start over under the palm trees? Life with no yearly winter snow in a sunny paradise. The dream ended when a tire blew, the SUV rolled, and the county coroner's office and Highway Patrol could not find any family to notify. Under those circumstances all that the officials could do was to store the personal effects for the statutory period pending any claims.

There was also a legal issue raised about the residency of the deceased couple. They had left their former state with the intent of living in the Golden State. Absent any change of mind along the way, they had arrived there and apparently intended to stay there. Therefore they were legal residents for a time albeit now deceased.

Aside from the possible legal question, with no known heirs to talk to, the few personal items recovered from the SUV were logged in to be stored for the time required by law after which time the things could be sold at public auction. Among the personal items that would not be sold were social security cards and drivers licenses. So the items were stored in the unlikely event anyone ever showed up to claim them. How a couple of the items happened to get from a supposedly secure storage area to us at General Delivery, Auke Bay, Alaska, 99821 was a place we didn't want to go. If an attorney in San Diego didn't ask us about a roll of film, we would not ask about these items. Perhaps it had something to do with one of his poker nights. At least we each now had an Ohio driver's license to use in getting ones with the same names up here and social security numbers where any payroll deductions could go. If we were here long enough to think about jobs.

Which is how your mother, Mary Barnes Richmond, became known as Annie Evans in our life up here. And the former Barry Sanford, who you Richmond kids know as your father, Tom Richmond, is known around here as Hal Evans.

ERNIE - LOOKING BACK

I learned the more intimate details about how the photographer died through an unofficial source known as my weekly poker game with the guys from the local cop shop and some other buddies. Be sure they win some marginal hands, order burgers and beer, have a lot of fun. Exchange scuttlebutt about what is happening around town, in the courts, at the station house, and talk about who has been seen with whom without the relevant spouse. The hottest gossip was that the death at the airport had a twist borrowed from grade school lunch money extortion stories - the whirly. There was a lot of speculation that the decedent apparently didn't have some film with him in the hope that he could pick up some money above his contract price for taking certain pictures. What or who the pictures might be of was high-octane fuel for a lot of conjecture. As a well-known political figure with a reputation for seeking occasional feminine companionship outside home and hearth had been in town recently, the rumors were flying thick and fast.

The team sent by the photographer's concerned employers apparently assumed the film was in his car and made efforts to find out what rental car company he had used by taking immediate action. They dunked his head in and out of a stool in the men's room while flushing the toilet. A sign saying "Restroom Being Cleaned - Do Not Enter" kept out potential witnesses to this unusual shampoo. While the guy apparently eventually cooperated before the final whirl, he was held down too long and drowned.

The scene was dutifully recorded by a surveillance camera (a strange twist of fate) installed to check for unusual bathroom activities sometimes indulged in by people passing through. However, the dunkers were not caught full face as they bent over at their work. The dunkee's rental car was picked up out of the lot by the rental company and re-rented before the dunkers could find it and recover the film. The car was off somewhere either cruising the streets of San Diego or parked somewhere. Whoever was looking for it and the film would be checking motel parking areas and tourist attractions hoping to spot it. Checking the places that do fast photo processing most likely led them to the place where the clerk was killed. The team might even have been watching when film was dropped off by a couple driving a rental car of the right make and color.

All of this was, of course, just stuff floating around town until I got the phone call from my friend, Tom. I knew that he would call sooner or later during his vacation out here after he and Mary had enjoyed time away from kids and social schedules. What I didn't expect was a call for help. Even as I set on the deck that evening watching a standard fantastic San Diego sunset, I didn't connect the event on the evening news with him. Yet the tone of his voice on the phone when he called triggered the attorney response mode in me. The one where you realize that there is a problem, say something to calm things down, tell the person what they want to hear that will shift some of the load. In this case, my response was a combination of bad jokes and then instructions about where I would meet them. Take the immediate steps first. Then get the facts and decide what to do next.

In the law trade, you quickly learn never to be surprised by what comes your way from a client or the opposing attorney. Or a judge. At least not to show surprise unless doing so can help you. I learned this early on when my practice wasn't really a career. I was sent a legal aid case by the county bar. The young married woman had separated from her husband for whatever reason, such as his nervously loading and unloading a pistol during dinner times, and wondered if her child could be taken from her because of the separation. Though I had never appeared in court on that type of issue or, in fact, any other, I assured her that in most cases a child would stay with the mother as long as she could care and provide for the child properly. She accepted that and asked, "We have been separated for six months and filed for divorce. Can I go on a date?"

Again I assured her that a mere instance of a date should not be grounds for taking her child away. After all, at some point she would need to get on with her life.

She nodded her head, thought for a minute and asked, "What if I got pregnant on that one date?"

I thought for a moment and then told her that while it was not the ideal circumstances and I didn't think it would be cause for her to lose her child, it was not as easy to be positive.

She looked across the desk and said, "I just have one more question."

I said, "What might that be?"

She was silent for a then said, "What if the father-to-be is my stepbrother?"

I thought for a moment, then calmly said, "You may have a slight problem."

That was the start of my continuing legal education. Even when your client's toupee falls off while he is testifying, just continue unless acknowledging it would advance your case. 'Hair today, gone tomorrow' might not be an appropriate observation.

The fact that my friend would be the one to have a roll of film, find a murder victim, and be on the run seems only to prove that lightning, or an earthly version of it, can strike twice. I first met my friend Tom over twenty years ago while doing my service time as an ensign assigned to the Pacific Fleet Headquarters offices in San Diego. Family connections got me assigned there though I had not sought the help. As the brass knew that I was not on a career track, I caught the semi-legal assignments there that were not for the upward bound ring-bearers. One such detail was to take a staff car and meet an arriving navy recruit named Tom Richmond at the San Diego Airport. I was ordered to be sure that he got inside the fence at the Navy Recruit Depot.

My normal pre-military response would have been to inquire why he was different from any other recruit. They come in groups and are normally met by a steely-eyed chief who gets their military careers off to a proper start. I may have looked like I had a question but was told, "Do it, do it right, and do phone in a report to the Chief of Staff's aide. Nothing goes on paper."

Except that it happened on a day after I had 'reported for duty' at the family home in La Jolla for the weekly dinner with my parents. There were, of course, the usual questions about my post-navy plans and when did I plan to join the family law firm. Corporate law and/or estate planning did not seem to be something I wanted to do. Not questions about when Karen and I might bless them with a grandchild but how soon I could start putting in what would be eighty-hour weeks to avoid questions of preferential treatment. After dinner, while waiting in the library for Dad to finish a call while Karen and Mom were out on the deck, I browsed the day's New York Times. One of the major stories in the local news section came to mind the next day as the passenger I was to escort came off the flight from the East Coast. The young guy was accompanied by a guy wearing an off-the-rack suit, shoes that needed to be polished, and a tie that maybe dated back to some long-ago Christmas. He and a young guy headed directly for me as he said, "Ensign Anderson? Initial this form. The package is yours. I need to catch a flight headed east. Have a nice day."

With that, he picked up his carry-on bag and left. A ship passing in the night except that it was a sunny day. I introduced myself to the recruit, Tom Richmond, welcomed him to San Diego and said, "I have a staff car parked outside. If you need to shop, snack or take a break, just say so."

He looked around the terminal and said, "My escort didn't have much to say. Ten words in almost three thousand miles is not much conversation. Maybe a burger and coke before you drop off what he referred to as the package would be nice."

Which is how we met all those year ago. After
we had the burger break and chatted in general
terms, I dropped him off at the Navy Recruit Depot
as ordered, returned to my duty station, and made
the phone call to the aide to the Chief of Staff.
Mission accomplished. I finished my two years of
obligated ROTC active duty time.   The recruit
finished his basic training and served his enlistment
in San Diego. We kept in touch. He would from
time to time come to our house for dinner with his
latest flame. It was like my wife and I were sort of a
quasi family for him though we weren't that much
older. He didn't say much about his past even when
I used my nearly subtle legal efforts to pry. Then he
was discharged and returned to the Mid-West to go
to college. My private practice, mostly not corporate
and not estate planning was doing well when he
called a few years later to invite me to his and Mary's
wedding. We went and had a wonderful time though
there was no one there from his side of the family,
just navy and college buddies.   Mary had family
there though they were not many in number due to
age and social commitments in their retirement
communities. It has been a good friendship over the
years, god parenting and all. Though I have always
wondered about what I read in the New York Times
that night before I picked up the package at the San
Diego Airport, I have never asked him about it.

FROM THE OVAL OFFICE

I can't say that nobody never ever warned me that my wandering eye might lead to times of trouble. Even my dear mother, God rest her sainted soul, tried her best in her gentle way to slow me down starting when I was only eight or nine years old. That reserved and gracious lady of the Older South seemed to intuitively know where I was headed. Maybe it all started even earlier when I was chasing the little blond girl under the quilting frame when I was only four or five while the needles above came and went as gossip and wisdom were passed around the table. I didn't know why I was so intent on chasing her; it just seemed the right thing to do.

Or perhaps it was what me and a neighbor girl tried to figure out in her backyard playhouse a year or two later. Well, we were just playing house was my explanation when questions were asked later. She had told her sister about how we played. The sister felt the duty of a sister was to tell her mother. That led to my first talking to and about the unspoken subject with the not saying much in detail that was common back then. Of course, as a result, the longer I was in school, the greater my interest in knowing more details became.

Of course, in the Good Ol' Boy South, filled with budding belles, there was a heap of learning to do outside of schoolwork. Maybe the ways I learned to gain more knowledge about what was becoming my favorite pastime also made me a good politician later on. After all, both careers involve a lot of people skills, creating trust, making promises you can't always keep or maybe never intended to.

I learned fast and well and thoroughly enjoyed the process. It was almost like I had a natural talent for it. Some folks are good at tinkering with cars and some with tools. And as with any other well-developed skill, it needs to be honed from time to time to keep doing it well. Of course, like the stock car drivers in our part of the country, you accept the risk involved as part of the game. Even after marriage and being further up the ladder toward your bigger goal. My political mentors along the long path to this office often played the same game I did, were more or less skillful, but had less to lose if the odds caught up with them. They, knowing me, tried to lessen the risk but were not always able to slow me down.

With the high level of security at the White House combined with the packed schedule, even the occasional opportunity to really explore a new female venue is rare though it has been done. The wife and kids kept coming and going so I was generally walking the straight and narrow during most of the first four years regardless of what the press constantly hinted at.

With the first four years ending, the time came to try for the second brass ring. It seemed like a sure thing but still had to be carefully managed. Then during the long week of convention pressure, seeing that pretty face in the front row was a way to mentally slip away from the noise and clamor. After the final speech was made with the crowds exiting and the lights dimming, it was time for my chance to relax. A few words quietly spoken set the wheels in motion.

TESTIMONY:

SECRET HEARING OF THE SENATE SELECT COMMITTEE ON PRESIDENTIAL SECURITY

The day after the presidential party returned to Washington, a meeting of the little known group charged with overseeing presidential security was held. As such meetings needed to be held without alerting the ever-vigilant press, which sometimes uncovers news without the aid of a press briefing, it was ostensibly held as a prayer breakfast in a private dining area. The cover was accurate in the sense that some of the members were praying that nothing more serious than a nomination had happened in San Diego.

The sole item on the unpublished agenda was to hear the basics of what might be considered a security breach by some and by others as just a bump in the road of middle age hormones asserting themselves. The view depended on which side of the political divide the person happened to be on. Membership on the committee was not considered a plum assignment like being on Appropriations or Judiciary but rather as a way to get time in grade toward eventual membership on something with more prestige. The chairman had been waiting over twenty years for a chance to move on and still had faint hope that it might happen. A committee where hearings were held in secret and there was no television coverage didn't do much for letting the folks back home know how hard you were working for them.

In the absence of media coverage, the members were even restrained in political posturing and did not wear the somber for constituent faces they might have otherwise affected. The looks of indignation when the story was told were saved for more public times. The chairman even left his down-on-the-nose trademark glasses off.

The only witness to be heard was the Secret Service agent in charge of the presidential security detail at the recent convention. How pictures were apparently taken of the Commander in Chief in a possibly compromising situation was still being looked into although a complete and accurate answer most likely would never be known.

After the chairman called the committee to order, the witness was called and sworn in. His testimony was brief.

"I was the agent in charge of the convention security detail at the hotel in San Diego when this incident occurred. Our agency has a solid reputation for doing its job of not only protecting the physical being of our client but also the privacy of what goes on behind the scenes of his public and private life. So what I will say behind these closed doors and within those parameters is that we did and continue to do our job quite well. We can't guarantee total success what with all the weirdoes out there but we really do a first class job overall.

"We do our best to recognize risks and dangers, to anticipate such things and take appropriate action. Yet sometimes things get beyond our abilities, especially when our boss, the commander in chief, won't listen. Then you have to minimize the risk as much as possible and hope for the best.

"In this matter, our team was - and has been for several years - dealing with the highest hormone level of anyone we had been charged with since the early sixties. We were also fully aware of the potential consequences, physical and otherwise, particularly because of the home and hearth platitudes promoted during his first term in spite of some colorful accusations made by parties he had encountered during his rise to power.

"Before we left for San Diego, Rambler was constantly on the go preparing for the convention even though the results were already known. The stress level was a maximum for him and for us. Then during the whole week of the convention in San Diego, there was one very dynamic lady that seemed to be at every rally and always within view of the incumbent when he was on the floor. She had long reddish hair, great legs, certainly not flat-chested but not overwhelming, very nicely dressed with lots of fine points that kept even the most stoic guys on our team aware of her. Of course, you can imagine what happened over the week of activities as our charge noticed her coming and going. Our team went on high alert waiting for something to happen. It was therefore no surprise when after the convention formalities were done that Rambler quietly suggested that the lady might like to meet him.

"We always, as you know, reserve an entire floor wherever we travel with our charge. Which means extra rooms one can duck into to use for private chats with various factions. You can perhaps fill in the details of what had taken place during the week: eye contact, a brief smile, an implied suggestion that perhaps that lady would like to meet him - and he would like to meet her.

"That's how, late one night, after the long day ended as the party had planned with the re-nomination in place, speeches made, all the party faithful dealt with, a meeting took place, some pleasantries were exchanged, and there was a definite increase in the temperature in that room even in front of the agent who watched the proceedings. All this, of course, with the rest of the family preparing for bed just six doors away.

"We had taken the best precautions we could, metal detector, pat-down search and so forth. Except for the routine checks made on all convention delegates and alternates, we had no chance to do even a really thorough check on the new friend who had somehow managed to be part of the convention. We still have not been able to find out how that specific candid camera got into the room. It was apparently inductance actuated by body mass which is somewhat like what sets off automatic toilet flushers that you may have contended with. The room had been searched, swept for bugs, all that, several times that day.

"Yet we now believe the film apparently shows that after the introductions and some very brief casual talk, the first swift moves and an embrace were followed by the initial grope. Then came complete utter surprise when Rambler's hand came back after finding clear evidence that the beautiful lady wasn't a she. What we suddenly had was a same sex relationship. It was the first time that something like this ever happened in our work. J. Edgar Hoover was probably rolling over in his grave laughing. What he could have, would have, done with this.

"The immediate problem for our people was to establish a perimeter, keep the lid on, get the 'lady' out of there but not to where 'she' could talk, all of this going into motion while the leader of the free world is lamenting about how he could not believe what he had just grabbed.

"Of course we quickly escorted the guy, high heels and all out, had her/him put on ice by transferring him between local police stations while trying to decide how to keep his story from being sold to the highest bidder. Then, as his purse had produced a New Jersey driver's license, it seemed that federal laws about crossing state lines to commit a crime might apply. Yet what crime had been committed? Misrepresentation? Before long 'he' was confined to the most remote area of the federal facility in San Diego.

"Shortly after that is when we found the rigged camera minus film and started our own search for the roll. It took us almost a whole day to do all the leg work at local rental places before we tied in the film to a death at the airport and to a car that was picked up there by a rental company.

"By that time it had been serviced, cleaned, and was back somewhere on the streets of San Diego. Or elsewhere. And the 'lady' had been sprung on bail and killed. Which seems senseless, in retrospect, because even without the film, she/he could be just as useful in exerting leverage. I still have nightmares imagining her/him as a guest on one of the late night talk shows.

"Anyway, all of our dedicated, professional efforts finally produced results more by chance rather than skill. The rental car was spotted out toward the beach areas leaving the scene of a crime. A murder, in fact. And one of our units just happened to have arrived at the same place while checking photo-processing places just in case the film was turned in for developing along with other film. The current renters of the car, probably being tourists, might have turned the roll in with their own film.

"That's how we first were able to find out what they looked like. They were just an average early middle-aged couple, nothing unusual, and apparently completely unaware of what was on the roll of film that was left in the car they had rented. And when the guy left the photo place, our agent could see from the vehicle we were using that something in the shop had really hit him hard. He left so fast that he almost hit our unit.

"That's when our agent called for another unit to cover the photo place and watch what was going on while he followed the rental car down the street till it stopped in another shopping mall.

"The guy barfed on the pavement before he and his wife walked to a burger place. Of course our agent hung back while the local police caught up and did their number. But their search did not locate the couple. Our guy lost them when the bus they had boarded crossed through the light at Pacific Highway and got over the railroad crossing just before the gate came down."

After finishing his testimony, the witness was asked a few questions and then instructed to wait outside in case the committee had any more questions. As he left there were murmurings of 'here we go again' and 'anytime anything happens.'

The committee members set as quietly as committee members ever do when the chairman pounded his gavel to get their attention. As the chairman, he felt that it was his duty to get in the first words and set the tone for any discussion. He led off with a short speech which by Washington standards set a record for brevity. "We are, once again, beset by the concept of security failure, or at least lapse, or at the very least a breach to some extent, the full extent of which must be ultimately determined, if that is possible, and which situation being brought about by the person being protected, who, in turn, has the ultimate authority and/or right to authorize and allow such a breach."

His colleagues seemed awed by the careful words which would have sounded almost comical outside of Washington or a comedy skit.

He continued, "But by exercising that option, or right, or right of free choice, he exposed, no pun intended under the stated circumstances, the country, our country, to potential lowering of world esteem, depending on the part of the world and the culture involved. That, of course, is aside from any physical danger of any potential type. We must, of course, remember that the security people are held responsible for one type of physical danger but not necessarily the other." As the monolog continued, one foolhardy committee member finally stood up and requested a point of order. While it was not the correct parliamentary procedure, the chair paused just long enough for the errant member to ask, "Does our leader know that his conduct could cause us to lose our jobs in the next election and have to return to living in communities we are no longer a part of?"

The Chairman replied, "I'm not going to be the one to tell him that."

With that, he called the witness back into the room, reminded him that he was still under oath, and said, in a complete switch from his prior pedantic style, "You folks had to let this happen. While you were following orders of the commander in chief, orders are just that. Orders. Not an instruction to allow some foolishness. Things happen along the way that delay or prevent carrying out orders. I'm sure that if the First Lady had been standing in the hall, you people would have been able to change directions, not parade the visitor past her. So, your agency gets the task of finding the film and destroying it or any negatives and prints. Let us know when that is done."

THE PHOTO OP

She came into the room followed by the ever-present Secret Service agent. Her walk suggested breeding, perhaps innate, perhaps learned at one of the better Eastern woman's finishing schools. The blouse and long skirt looked as though they came from one of the up-scale shops in La Jolla. Shoulder -length auburn hair glinted in the light from the floor lamps as she came toward me. A faint hint of La Enchantress accompanied her. She seemed perfectly at ease in meeting me - lots of people I meet seemed to be blinded by the light of the office I hold. Yet even in her ease there seemed to be a hint of fun to come.

I stood up as she walked toward me even as I felt myself starting to spring to attention. I'm sure Mae West could have delivered a great line about my condition. The Secret Service guy kept his gaze straight ahead, level and alert just as I was. Oh well, it just made it very clear what we were here for, in a sense pointed out our agenda.

So after about ten seconds of social stuff like introductions I suggested to Roberta that she sit down on the sofa. And, of course, I immediately sat down next to her on her right. This sort of Plan A strategy gave me an opportunity for my left arm to go casually behind the lady and left the right arm and hand free to roam. Which I did by a slow sweep from her knee upward along her panty hose.

Sensing no objection, I went further along the path. As I edged closer to my goal, the realization came that what I had expected to find was not there and that what was there was not what I had expected to find. That was when she unsnapped her skirt and pulled it back to expose the emerging scene. My hand froze in place for a few long seconds before I let loose of my discovery and then retreated much faster than it had advanced. I remember looking at the hand as it emerged from the center of where the skirt had been. I may have said something graphically profound like, "Imagine that."

Roberta smiled and said "Are we having fun yet? Hi. I'm Robert." I stood up, my left hand now clutching my right wrist, turned to the Secret Service agent, and said "Please see our guest out." Perhaps I should have said something like "You all take care now" or "Nice meeting you" but certainly not "You all come back now." Yet I was as confused as a hound dog with possums running off in three different directions.

After that, I set in silence for several very long minutes before thoroughly washing my hands and heading back to the family suite. It surely had been a long day.

AGENT REPORT -

"ONLY THE MAINTENANCE MAN"

I had been detailed by the agent in charge of our detail to introduce Miss X to our charge, code name Rambler. The code name was not selected because of his storytelling ability but based on other talents. This was not the first such scenario of this type - fortunately the times have become fewer lately - and certainly another event to be filed away under 'never to be discussed.' Short of a strip search, all the security steps possible on short notice had been taken before Miss X was handed over to me. When the elevator doors opened, the agent who had escorted her up to our floor managed to conceal a smile as he said, "This is the guest that the president is expecting."

I wondered if a lady would be visiting this late if she was less attractive.

We moved quickly down the hall past the room where the rest of the presidential family was supposedly sleeping. When I entered the room with the guest, things moved really fast even for Rambler. They went from introductions to the couch to his moves in an almost continuous flow. I remember that she had pulled open her skirt when he suddenly pulled his hand back, looked at it for several seconds, looked at me, then stood up and asked me to see the lady out.

The words and the tone he used as his left hand clutched his right wrist alerted me to some problem so, as standard protocol, I radioed ahead to the other agents on duty to go slow in escorting the lady out. After handing the lady over to the next agent, I headed back to the room where Rambler was still sitting. I asked if there was a problem. He said only "He hasn't had any surgery yet. What a surprise. Let's take steps to keep this from the press." Which is what we tried to do but someone bailed the guy out and he ended up in a dumpster south of Broadway dead as a losing lottery ticket.

After Rambler left to go to his room, the agent in charge cornered me in the hall and told me what I could have guessed. He said, "Rambler is concerned about his public image if this gets out."

I replied, "I understand. We will do what's necessary to keep a lid on it. Any idea why the scam?"

He answered, "I don't know yet. Maybe it's just an attempt by the tabloids to get something else for the masses to speculate on."

"Don't they like to run front page photos of the latest find at Area 57?," was my question.

"Yes," he answered. "Is there any chance that pictures were taken?"

"Pictures?" I replied.

"Yes," he came back with. "Remember those cheap freebie cameras that we strongly objected to having placed in every room?"

"Oh, my God, you don't think...," I blurted out.

"Yes, I do," he said. "Anyone but you, Rambler, and the guest in that room?"

I answered, "Only the maintenance guy checking smoke alarm batteries after Rambler left. Oh, shit."

THE FIRST LADY

By now, after all the years we have been in politics, I should be used to the late nights and lack of details about what is going on around me. I did think that after the convention there might be a few hours when the family could come first before starting on the campaign trail marathon. Yet when the official public part of the evening and celebration ended, he was off again to meetings up and down the hall. That, of course, was as one hundred per cent as predictable as the next tabloid tale about his latest side trip down the street of middle age dreams. We, the kids and I, got a quick goodnight and a promise to be back in an hour or so. Four years from now, if we hold up, it should all be over. Except for the young elder statesman role that he will have to undertake.

Anyway, when he did finally get back to the room, he seemed different somehow. Subdued perhaps, not just from being exhausted by the past week and past three years in office. It was as if he had turned a corner in his life but did not want to talk about it. Perhaps talking, at least to me, wasn't really necessary anyway.

WHAT, ME WORRY?

The real potential downside of what had happened as a result of my impulsive act of gonaditis began to dawn on me as we prepared to fly back to Washington the next day. The family was packed up and ready though the kids had wanted to stay a few more days in the sun. I was ready to head out of Dodge and think about world issues and re-election rather than the recent event. The morning security briefing and other meetings had helped me focus a bit. At least my mind was diverted for a few minutes from worrying about whether Roberta/Robert would be front page news that day or sprung on me at some time in the future.

I had been assured by my security detail that the matter was under control and that I was not to worry. Roberta/Robert was a guest at the federal detention center and if the camera had film in it, the film would be found and all would be well. That logic made about as much sense as being told that the energizer bunny will run forever or that all attorneys are honest.

Finally we were ready to leave the hotel for the motorcade back to Air Force One. The local dignitaries (Read: Thanks for the many dollars your group has left with our local economy.) along with the top brass of the Committee to Re-elect America's President aka CRAP were standing by in front of the cameras ready to shake hands as we headed for the limo. As the TV cameras whirled, my mind raced wildly wondering what their reactions would be if they knew what else that hand had shaken recently. I somehow even managed to smile and wave as we moved quickly toward the limo though I was operating on automatic while trying to look presidential.

Later, in the air, I began to ponder what impact any exposure of my exposure might have. After all, I am paid to meet and greet and schmooze with world leaders of every nation, belief and culture. What about the Middle East places where one hand is dedicated to eating and one for other chores related to the body? Could I keep a straight face in those situations? And what about the forthcoming campaign where 'pressing the flesh' as LBJ used to say was done by the hour day after day but in a different way?

Maybe what was really bothering me was not so much the physical aspect of what had happened. After all, I handle something like what I had grabbed several times a day but it's not hooked to some other guy and not one dressed like that one was. It's more the mental part of it, the being taken in, so completely fooled. Guilt I can deal with when I stray and get caught but being just plain taken in hurts. I felt like a rube at the county fair.

Well, I probably won't have to worry if the security aspect comes up before that Senate Committee on watching our watchdogs. What they hear they won't tell because if they tell, then I can tell about them, and more of them could lose. In Washington, the code of loyalty is more about wanting to be able to sin and knowing that what is known won't be used. Most of us know better than to party with an exotic dancer who takes a swim in a pool at the Tidal Basin while both parties are drunk. Things that public can't be kept quiet in a town like Washington where gossip is a way of life.

So even if only me, the 'lady,' and at least one agent knew the specifics of what happened, what would be the impact if the world knew? Not to mention what hours of fun the late night talk show hosts would have. Even more worrisome was what would happen if the First Lady, now dozing beside me, ever found out. That chill would go a long way toward ending global warming. All the other possible consequences might be minor compared to her reaction.

LT. BONK CARLSON - HOMICIDE DIVISION - SAN DIEGO POLICE DEPARTMENT

At age 40, Lt. Robert 'Bonk' Carlson knew that no matter how good he was at tracking down various killers that crossed his path, amateur and otherwise, he would live the rest of his life with his nickname. Even now, while conducting a morning briefing for his detectives on the murders of the day, his mind flashed back to how it had happened.

Back to when eighteen years younger and twenty pounds lighter, he had been a star receiver on the San Diego State football team. The Aztecs had come to the last play of the last game of the season locked in a tie. The winners would collect all the marbles: conference championship, a possible trip to a bowl game, and maybe even pro offers for some of them.

With seconds left on the clock, the quarterback called for the Hail Mary pass, everyone possible down field, and go for the big bomb. He remembered the snap, the effort to out step and outrun his coverage as he ran a perfect pattern down toward the goal line. Then a lowering of his head and a last feint as he came to where the ball would be if he was the intended receiver. And ran head-on into the goalpost.

The roar of the crowd died to a stunned silence as he bounced back from the impact staggering to remain on his feet. The 'bonk' from hitting the post seemed to be the only sound in the stadium. As he wobbled in a daze he threw his arms up and out trying to stay on his feet. The ball, having been launched before the collision, floated down right on its intended course and into his outstretched arms. Somehow he grabbed onto it, clutched it, and fell forward across the goal line.

The crowd roared back into life, the game was won, and he became forever Bonk.

Now he stood before his men thinking that times were certainly easier back then even with the mild concussion he had suffered from the impact. He had thought that when the convention was over things would get back to normal for the department. There would be no more extra shifts providing security and watching over high profile tourists. Instead the pace had quickened rather than slowed. Along with the usual weekend quota of violent deaths of locals and visitors by knife, guns, drugs, and other normal means, there had been the ugly scene at the photo shop to deal with. It was the first murder he had ever encountered that involved a tripod as the apparent weapon. Motive so far was lacking. And the fact that the victim was a shirttail relative of the chief was sure to bring extra heat on the division.

Then there was the one out at the airport. That victim, still to be identified, seemed to have hidden something that the killers wanted quite badly. Drowning in a public commode was a gruesome way to check out. The video of the murder should help in solving that one. The South of Broadway victim strangled with his bra and left in a dumpster seemed tame by comparison. And to top it off, some of the federal folks from the security detail for the president seemed to be staying in town longer than their work required. Maybe there was something going on that was not the subject of interagency cooperation. Right now though, the need was to get on with the efforts to locate the couple that had been seen leaving the parking lot near the photo shop just before the first police unit arrived. Even if they were not involved, they might have witnessed something that would lead to the killer or killers. The clerk had at least managed to trigger the silent alarm before her death; maybe that was why she had been killed so brutally. Time now, however, to deploy the troops and get on with the business of the day. There was also the question of why the Secret Service units were seen at the photo shop and around the abandoned rental car if they were not involved in anything. It would be a weird form of sightseeing.

THE BOARD MEETING

The Board of Directors of Roberts Interstate Cooperative Operations, commonly called RICO in deference to the federal law designed to act against organized criminal activities that cross state lines, met in a duly called special meeting shortly after the post-convention events in San Diego. The purpose for the special meeting was to discuss the aftermath of the photography project and to decide how to proceed.

Having reorganized the corporate structure of the national organization after a meeting years earlier at a New Jersey estate resulted in overtime pay for every lawman in the area, the current management operated more under Robert's Rules Of Order than the former hierarchy had felt necessary.

The meeting was held in the boardroom at the national headquarters in Washington, DC. The headquarters location had been selected so that it could be close to the nation's capital as a sort of unofficial arm of national policy. After the chairman called the meeting to order a report on the San Diego project was made by the Director of Planning and Operations for the Western Region. The report covered the origin of the project which was to develop and implement a plan that would provide leverage in the next presidential administration. In essence, as one of the more blunt directors had put it earlier, "We want to get a hook in that will make it possible for us to do our business with less interference from the Justice Department."

The plan that had been decided on after consideration of several alternative proposals was to place the President in such a position that the risk of public ridicule could be discretely used to soften what his appointees might do while in office. "After all", as one blunt director had said, "We put him in a spot where it goes beyond a quick roll in the hay. That, given what people accept now, might lose him a few votes in Peoria. We want something that, if it was made public, would make it almost impossible for him to deal seriously with world leaders if they knew of the event. The handshake that is so important in showing solidarity and mutual respect when world leaders meet becomes a laugh in connection with his administration."

Another director was recognized by the chair and stated, "It's basic leverage, the corporate equivalent of what used to done with muscle. Now it's called finesse. Our lobbyists explain our views to the right people who can let the president know our position. Then he can remember to lean our direction in his policy-making."

The report submitted on the project indicated that the plan had been organized, funded, and carried out with utter precision until there had been a disagreement over the contract price for photographic services. The three employees seeking to resolve the dispute exceeded their authority to negotiate and terminated the talks by killing the photographer. They also made an unplanned appearance on a video camera. The fiasco illustrated the problems inherent in following federal law regarding rehiring and retraining of employees after long periods of unemployment when the employee is unable to report for work due to work related activities. Two of the team members had served lengthy prison terms for carrying out company business. During that time the organization had abandoned most of the strong arm tactics previously used. Two of the San Diego murders might have been avoided if the team had followed negotiation techniques now taught.

Before regional management was able to call the team off, another foul-up had resulted in a second death. That was followed by a third fatality as the team blundered along seeking to cover their tracks. At that point the team was ordered out of the area and 'Sunshine' was brought in to do damage control, i.e. locate the missing film and take any necessary action against those having it.

SUNSHINE

I do contract work for a national privately owned business organization in a job that offers steady and interesting work, an opportunity to travel to new places for assignments of varying length, more than adequate income to support my family along with a performance bonus program, and a great retirement plan. The company also pays for membership in an industry trade group and for ongoing educational programs where one can learn the latest techniques of the trade.

Even with all the perks, what I really resent is that the public refers to a person in my line of work as a 'hit man.' That raises an unwarranted image of callous violence and pain, the rattle of automatic weapons, storm and drama like on most television programs including the evening news. While those traits may be typical of many of the less skilled in this profession, we, I, prefer to think of my profession as being that of a dispatcher. A job needs to be done, the intended target is located and, if necessary, dispatched in a quiet, painless, and unobtrusive way. If done with proper professional skill, the only public notice will be an obituary in the local paper. The targets were not your average John Does as when a husband or wife wants out and fears the property settlement consequences or wants to collect on the big new life insurance policy. It would more likely be a high living drug lord making the business look bad or a politician who went beyond acceptable levels of corruption. Sometimes people in government would need to stop a terrorist threat in a discreet manner. Then there were the supposedly necessary regime changes around the world to ensure that one nation lived up to the high standards set by another. Sometimes I wondered whether what I did made any sense or any difference.

On this assignment, I started well below the power curve. That made it even more of a challenge for my talents. Some real clowns had left bloody and wet tracks around San Diego, which had caused the people I needed to do my business with to take cover. By the time I had placed the project I was doing on hold and taken a flight to San Diego, the subjects were well hidden or had left the area. The home office had confirmed that they had not contacted their children or used any credit card or telephone card. We decided not to take any action against their kids until and unless that leverage was needed. Dealing directly with the parents would leave less tracks.

I called my wife and told her my trip had been extended for an unknown time. I said goodnight to her and promised to bring her something special from San Diego. At that time I did not know how far this assignment would take me and her.

Then I mentally charted my plan of action. It makes the work much more interesting when the target is difficult to locate. First I would get a few feelers out to see what the local police and the feds might be doing. Than do the background research on the subjects. That would probably involve a trip to their home town. The important part is to know everything possible and more about their lives and personal habits and traits. You need to know everything down to the brand of underwear worn, the type of shampoo used, and even the type of coffee or tea they like and what they put in it. Get enough details and anyone can be found as this couple would be.

When I do locate and identify them, I will either recover the film or find out where it is. I don't know why the film is important and don't really care. TMI - too much information - can make the job harder at times. If necessary, I will quietly resolve any threat to my client's business plan. Perhaps along the way, I can arrange to have my signature tune played on local radio stations. Once they know that 'Sunshine' is looking for them, hearing "Everywhere you go, sunshine follows you" might put them off balance enough to make a slip.

THE PHOTOGRAPHER

I get my assignments through a referral service. A lot of the work is routine, shoot shots of a landscape or a building or something else for an ad campaign or a brochure. What I really like to do is the other stuff when it involves a little more agility to keep from getting punched by the subject and having your nose or camera broken. It also helps at times to be able to run fast when the person becomes aware of your presence.

The way it works, a company (read: tabloid newspaper) wanting action shots of a person, place or event the person is involved in calls the service. The request is matched to the next person on the list for an assignment unless a specific name is requested. All of us on the list do this freelance work even though we may have regular jobs to fill in between going on the road. We have to be inventive enough to figure how to get the shot like of the royals frolicking, the toe kiss, that sort of stuff. I also do some industrial work like trying to catch the new cars before they get to the showroom.

Anyway, this assignment promised to be a bit more difficult what with the Secret Service hanging around so tight. The security around the subject would be top level. Somehow I needed to have access to the rooms where the main players would be staying and holding their private meetings. Maybe I could get on the hotel payroll. It only took one phone call properly worded to get a full credit report on the hiring guy at the hotel. There were some recent very high interest loans he had acquired along with a similar pattern in the past. A few bucks invested with a local private eye type showed that there were frequent trips south of the border to the dog track and seasonal jaunts up to Del Mar to watch the ponies run. These hobbies led to an ongoing need for extra cash. An unwritten part of his latest loan application promised that it would be interest free if he agreed to put a new hotel maintenance guy on the payroll. Me. Problem solved. With that taken care of, I decided that something to do with the smoke alarm might be the way to go to get access to the hotel rooms. I spent some very boring hours running down nine-volt batteries. The idea was to get into the suite of rooms before the first security check. Install a battery that would go flat in two or three days and start to chirp which would then result in a call to the hotel management to fix it. A guy in hotel coveralls with proper identification shows up to replace the battery. While that was being done, a small mostly plastic camera with a simple remote could be planted. During the first battery switch, I would pick some likely spots like a pillow on a sofa, maybe in the place where spare blankets and pillows are stored. It had to be quick with a minimum chance of being noticed and so obvious that the place would not be searched.

The really neat part of the scheme was that a camera like the one I was to use would already be in the room; all I would need to do was a swap for my specially equipped model - the one with a remote. As a courtesy and of course as a business promotion, every delegate and every room was given a basic camera by a national company to record their role in history. I don't know how many markers were called in to arrange that and I didn't ask. It just made my life a lot easier.

The other element would be timing the shots without seeing what was happening. Allow time for the entry of the bait, some introductory words, and hope that the subject and his new friend would not waste any time getting acquainted. Given the track record of the subject, that was the easiest part of the job. I managed to solve the technical aspects by borrowing motion sensor technology that uses the presence and movement of two or more people to set off an exposure cycle for the camera. Every motion sets off an exposure and exposure was what I wanted pictures of.

After the photo session when the parties have left, another visit by hotel maintenance to recheck the smoke alarm battery and out with the film. No one knows what has happened till the next issue of the paper.

Then there was the matter of the bait. I did not arrange for that but knew the plan. A lady would show up, meet the subject, and I was to get face and crotch shots that could be used for publication or for leverage. Mine not to reason why, only do a professional job. Which I did with everything going without a hitch up to and including recovering the film. However when I saw the 'lady' being escorted out of the suite adjusting his bra, I decided that perhaps my services were worth more than the agreed price.

When I got to the airport where the film was to be picked up from me, I left my rental car in the return lot but did not check it in. I figured nothing would happen till I turned in the papers on it. In the meantime, I could meet the customers and firmly talk about more money. That was an error in judgment on my part. They were not willing to consider a change in price and proceeded to demand the film. I held firm. They proceeded to be firm also by holding me and giving me a close-up look at how the water flushes out of a toilet bowl. That convinced me that they were serious about the contract terms and I finally told them where the film was. Of course by then I was going down into the stool for the third or fourth time, not enjoying the view, and feeling drained. My last thought was something about thinking that this scene should be on film.

ROBERT(A)

If my golf buddies ever knew what I really do for a living, it would probably cause a lot of laughter and bad jokes - after a period of stunned silence. Perhaps it might even cause a little bit of introspection by a few of them; the others would most likely just write me off and move on in lock-step with their rigid, conventional myopia.

As far as they know, I work in the city for a major manufacturer of women's clothing and take occasional sales trips. I have a wife, two kids, and am a ten-handicap golfer. Probably the reason that the unseen part of my career has never crossed paths with their lives is that they are avidly heterosexual, beer drinking, sports watching macho males who can't conceive of any other world outside of their own.

While I am unabashedly 'straight' as my wife can readily confirm, my background and talents in art, acting, and design led me to a career in fashion, design, and motivational speaking. My presentations are always done in the female role so that the full impact of what is possible comes through. I present them at a few highly attended conferences each year under the theme of "Dressing For Success" which covers both the dressing and decorum necessary for males to achieve true feminine status.

The concept, which came about while watching "Some Like It Hot" a few years ago, is about how to dress and groom in a new role so the transformation is complete while also appearing totally natural. Obviously it involves going far beyond careful use of a razor and donning of a wig or hairpiece plus gender specific clothing. To be really out, over and accepted, the end creation has to pass the eyes of the most discerning male who does not doubt the gender of who he thinks he is really talking to. It must also be possible to be accepted among women without question. The changes can't be achieved in just a few hours, but come only with practice and real effort. Voice lessons help also.

The fact that I can travel in either gender without difficulty makes me a master/mistress of the art. Most of my training seminars are held on the West Coast, far from home. My wife is fully aware of this part of my work and understands why it is needed in our society. Although the surgical aspects of gender transformation have been dealt with, the more readily visible necessities of transformation have not been worked out quite as well. My opening line to set the theme is often about the man who underwent the transformation by surgery and later became a nun. That was the first transistor.

I had never thought of doing anything like I was asked to do in San Diego. However, a Traffic and Shipping Manager for a major firm importing merchandise from Canada was out in the Pacific Northwest in a coastal city studying methods to more efficiently ship merchandise by small boat without detection. A conference I spoke at was being held there in Port Angeles because of the more accepting and open-minded citizens there than in many major cities. He read about the convention that I was speaking at and contacted my agent after talking to his home office.

The money offered was substantial and if I could get by the guy that was being setup, it would be a real feather in my cap. Being able to pass an initial examination by such a known judge of femininity would put me at the top of my field. It would really show the value of grooming and dressing and what could be achieved. I didn't know that filming was involved and did not see any danger in doing what was proposed. I understood that it was a practical joke by the inner circle of a guy who had a great sense of humor.

When I managed to successfully carry off the plan, it quickly became obvious that the Secret Service guys had not been clued in and were not very happy when my real gender became quite clear. The guy in the room and the others that were called in had absolutely no sense of humor. The only thing they could think of to do was to lock me up while they discussed their next move and how to cover up what they had not uncovered. They could not just let me go but had to go up their chain of command for further orders. I was hauled off to jail and booked for something called material misrepresentation which I don't even think is a crime. Politicians do it all the time and never get charged.

Fortunately someone showed up to bail me out and I was released. I caught a cab back to my hotel and was almost there when we stopped while police cleared an accident scene. I paid the driver and started to walk the last half block to the hotel entrance. And, just like in the movies, I was dragged into an alley and sexually assaulted. Or at least an effort was made. My role-playing was apparently too good. The attacker, realizing he had been fooled, went ballistic and choked me with my bra. If the Secret Service had not kept the protective gear I always carry, I might have lived to wonder if this would ever be something I could share with my golf buddies.

TESTIMONY CONTINUED

We - the agency - were stymied because if our people show a degree of interest, high or low or at all, in area happenings flags go up and the local law people wonder why the interest. Even our mere presence near the photo place raised a few questions that we were able to dodge. Our ongoing extra presence in San Diego was explained as staff training for future similar security details during the campaign. But why San Diego and nice weather for such training rather than Minneapolis in the summer? Our answer was that we were already here which raised the thought that the government does not usually operate in such a logical manner.

After losing the couple at the railroad crossing (Viva Amtrak), we were really starting from behind our own goal line. Naturally, all the steps were taken to check people leaving town. Among other things, we had people working the airport at the security checkpoints, some people down at the border on both sides, and even one person on every Amtrak train headed north. It may seem like a lot of time and money to locate two people. Yet we felt, in a sense, the future of the free world was in our hands-no pun intended.

The one step that seemed most likely to produce results was what we did at the Border Patrol checkpoints on the highways headed north toward Los Angeles. With their help, no details given by us, we ask them to watch for a couple of the approximate heights, weights, and ages without spooking them. When a 'possible' came through, they would 'bug' the car by putting a small locator transmitter under the rear bumper. You can imagine how many cars and couples were possibles. Most of the cars bugged got as far as Los Angeles, maybe as far as Sacramento but most of those returned back south very soon or were checked further and found not to be of interest.

One couple driving a Blazer and pulling a ski boat seemed a good bet but how would they have gotten a boat and a car? It was bugged anyway. That vehicle kept going north past Los Angeles but without the boat. That seemed odd to some extent. Not wanting to risk using a helicopter to get a closer look (a bit too obvious), we decided on the old crop-duster flyby trick. We were able to confirm that the vehicle was making a beeline north without many stops. There was still no confirmation that it was the people that we wanted to talk to.

Somewhere south of Sacramento, the couple must have wised up, maybe wondered why the plane wasn't dusting, maybe made a quick check for a bug. Maybe they had seen that Alfred Hitchcock movie years back. Anyway, as a result, our people spent a day running around Sacramento and Yolo counties trying to trace the signals. Then we found we were following a sheriff's car. The couple, meanwhile, were off in a Blazer, license unknown, one of how many the Chevy division of General Motors made that year of that color. How far north would they go and how many places could they park and find a different way to travel?

While the San Diego police had not given the identity of the couple other than as "a tourist couple at the scene whose rental car was later found apparently abandoned in a parking lot" and "being sought as possible witnesses to the photo shop murder" we had to use other sources and ways to learn who they were. We wanted to avoid direct contact with their kids as that might open more doors to our interest.

Our agency did get some photographs when one of our people, trained in discreet information gathering i.e. breaking and entering without leaving any traces, visited their home. If the stolen photographs had been forwarded with the report sent to San Diego rather than being filed away in an out box, they would have been of more use to us. That visit was when we had the first hint that someone else had been in the house ahead of us on a similar mission. An interesting sidelight of the visit was that of the prints that were taken, none led to any on file with the FBI. How could there not be any on file for any family member? And who else had been on the scene? We decided to continue our efforts to locate the subjects, get a reading on what they were doing, watch them, and try to retrieve the missing film. That would not have been necessary if we had thought more about picture taking when Rambler was moaning about his find and we were escorting his guest out. By the time we did look for film, it was missing in action. We did find rigged cameras in other rooms with the film still in them.

Then, while we were following our game plan in Seattle, at the motel and then at the Marine Highway System pier, we began to be more sure that someone was paralleling our efforts. In thinking about who that someone might be, the usual suspect and logical person was the shadowy person called Sunshine. Knowing that various unnamed governmental agencies have had occasion to use his talents through intermediaries, we began to wonder who was tailing who. We decided to send one of our people further north to look for the film and for the other person looking for it.

Only one of our people had actually seen the couple we were looking for and then only the husband as he had rushed out of the photo shop distraught and hurrying and very pale. Some distant photos had been taken as the man later barfed out of an open driver's door but those didn't help very much. Maybe the agent could have or should have stepped forward at that time to kindly help a fellow citizen. Or maybe he figured the lady in the car should be the one to offer a tissue. Yet maybe he figured correctly that helping might bring our agency into full focus on the evening news.

The particular agent was one of the people we get on loan occasionally from the CIA and the Federal Marshal's Office to help out when we are overextended on the Security Detail. He also happened to be the same unlucky person who had escorted Miss X to meet Rambler - and forgot to check for film before escorting the visitor out of the room. He also forgot to return some basic personal protection items which may have contributed to the death of Rambler's guest.

Considering that his decisions, however correct, now were now considered errors of judgment leading to the ongoing search, he seemed like the logical person to detail long term to Alaska to search there.

After clearing with the agency he was on loan from, he was instructed to pack for rain and snow and head north to Alaska.

WHY ME?

When it was suggested that I pack well and plan to be gone for a while, I didn't think that the assignment was one that I really deserved. Until that time, I had had a successful career at my home agency, albeit one that would never be public knowledge. However a career of being low profile in various foreign countries evaluating information others have collected does not really prepare one for the supposedly plum assignment of being loaned to the Secret Service for the POTUS Security Detail.

Those guys are much more out in public view, work extra long hours, and have to be ready to 'take one' for the boss if needed. Also, I have never felt comfortable wearing dark glasses inside or standing watch for long hours in hotel corridors. I did my best as the new guy on the block though most of my time was on the family protection part of the assignment.

At least that was the case until that night in San Diego as the convention was winding down. We were leaving the next day on the flight back to Washington and the family was in for the night except for Rambler. I was about to be relieved and go off duty when I was called on my radio and told to expect to work an extra hour or so. The key phrase in the call was "SIG" which I understood to mean "Silence is golden."

That's why I was not surprised when the elevator door down the corridor opened and I was introduced to "Roberta." I recalled seeing her over the past few days on the convention floor in full view of Rambler as he came and went as part of the convention process. It did not completely surprise me that she was the guest who was to meet Rambler. I had received enough briefing when assigned to the security detail to not be surprised that something like this might take place.

The agent with the lady told me that he had already completed the search of her and her purse per our guidelines and said for me to introduce her to Rambler. I knew which room down the hall he was waiting in so she and I headed there. I had quickly rechecked the room before she arrived and everything seemed in order. Rambler was ready to receive company and seemed in a relaxed but ready mood.

We walked in. I introduced her to Rambler and they quickly set down on a couch facing the entertainment center. Or maybe the couch was to be the entertainment center. I moved to a position behind the couch near the door and watched, ever alert behind my dark glasses. Somehow the room seemed to suddenly get warmer. About ten seconds later, I heard the snaps on her skirt unsnapping. I was thinking about how fast things were moving when, from where I stood, I saw a puzzled look on Rambler's face as he was now holding his right wrist with his left hand. That's when I heard the lady say something and heard Rambler asking me to see our guest out. Which I did.

Was what happened my fault? No, but as the agent watching it happen and the last one who might have prevented it, I would be the first in line when blame was placed. I took the next steps per the S.O.P., got the guest out, and went back to the room where Rambler was still sitting silently. Later, he left and I escorted him to the door of the family suite where another agent was stationed. That's when the agent in charge came up and we talked about what had happened and had the little discussion we did about pictures. Again, how was I to know about the hotel maintenance man and smoke alarm batteries?

That talk may had led the agent in charge to later decide that I would be a good person to spend some time checking photo shops around town and watching for a rental car. Someone else could watch over the First Lady and the kids for now. The fact that I happened to be outside of the photo shop was just another bit of less than perfect timing on my part. And my holding back at the barf scene seemed to be a good choice though I must admit maybe I could have gone on to the burger place and had a cold drink and watched the couple. But then I could not have been behind the bus they boarded and been blocked at the railroad crossing.

So why, as a result of things beyond my control, did I get an open-ended assignment to a place where I might not even speak the language?

BONK - LOOKING FOR THEM

We, the San Diego Police Department ("We Serve"), didn't consider the couple from the photo shop prime suspects, more as possible material witnesses to the bloody scene out in the Midway area. That scene of horror probably had a lot of store clerks who worked alone wondering if prints not being ready or poor service could cause something like that. The security camera at the shop got a better shot of the man who came in than it did of whoever used the tripod on the clerk. The question now was, in a town of over a million people and maybe that many more visitors (tourists is a word to be avoided), who were they and where? The rental car abandoned down on Rosecrans gave some early leads that led to two tourists who had not yet returned from their trip or returned the rental car as agreed. It seemed like a dead end for a while.

We did find the luggage that they had left in their motel room and got a warrant to search it but it didn't really tell us very much. Then, nothing official stated, but it looked like the feds had more than a passing interest in the case. They kept showing up just to chat without any valid reasons. And something was being bandied around about a county sheriff's car up in Northern California being stopped because someone had planted a bug on it and it was wanted back.

At this point, playing a hunch, I started investing some phone time calling in some favors owed me by my brethren in cities up north such as San Francisco, Portland and Seattle. San Francisco was most difficult because it's still in California and cars left in long-term parking at the airport would have - guess what - mostly California plates. But the idea in playing the hunch was to see if a car with San Diego ownership showed up, was later claimed, and returned south. It seemed a long shot but what else did we have? I realized that the couple were not just witnesses but could possibly have something of great value that could likely place them in extreme danger from other hunters. On the other hand, how much do I need or want to know? Would locating them really help to close the three local cases that the chief was ragging me about?

So, on routine patrols of the lots looking for stolen cars, a lot of numbers were punched in. A few San Diego cars owned by locals showed up at San Francisco International but were picked up by returning travelers and produced no leads. With Seattle, it was easier. There were not too many California plates found and only one where the license plate frames showed it to be from San Diego. It was picked up out of the lot the same day we heard about it and back in San Diego two days later. It was still not much to go on except that the registered owner happened to be a local attorney that I happen to share poker nights with. I wonder if he will flinch when I drop a bomb. But did the couple fly, drive, or float from Seattle? Or were they still there hiding somewhere among the everyday house folks?

DAD

Baby boomers might be the cliché applied to those of us now somewhere around fifty years old, our kids raised as much as they ever will be, no major health or financial or marital concerns. We, your Mom and I, had been married for almost twenty -three years when this different type of mid-life crisis came along. Our married life has been very good though there have been the usual good, bad, and kid days as we have enjoyed the years together. You kids helped make it a special life - at least during most of the time you were growing up. Yet even with all the sharing over the years with your mother, there is a bit of my past that I had never shared with her until that evening in San Diego.

As you guys know from many tellings, we met during our junior years back at one of those Mid-Western state cow colleges, the one that you have seen in our yearbooks. Actually it was a very good land grant college that later upgraded itself to university status. The fees were low if you were from in-state, which gave more education for the dollar. Which is different from what college costs now. Though not really from the state, I was headed for a degree in business and communications; she was planning to be a teacher. I was about three years older than her, having spent some time in the Navy along the way to college. She was the interviewee in an article I did for the campus daily about teaching as a potential career and how well our school prepared one for it.

Realizing that she was both attractive and intelligent, my interest was immediately raised. She did not seem to be one of the coeds of that era that came to college to get a quick Mrs. degree. Attractive without overstating her natural beauty, from a solid farm and family background in the western part of the state, she made sense when she talked. And as you kids know, Dad spoke carpe diem. We were married just after my graduation with the rest being our family history. Part of that history is that my parents had died in a tragic accident leaving me on my own at age eighteen to pursue time in the service before starting college. That leaves some blanks to be filled in which I have not done till now. My excuse was that I just wanted to forget the actual circumstances of how my folks died. Now the rest of the story.

My early life was the usual route for kids in the upper Midwest. My dad owned a local independent insurance agency which he had taken over when his father died. My mother ran the house which was what wives generally did in that era though times were a changing. Hot summers and cold winters year after year, family vacations, holiday celebrations, absolutely nothing remarkable until high school graduation finally arrived. I had shown some fledgling writing ability along with having a few small parts in school plays. I had considered the idea of perhaps seeking a career that might use those interests as I didn't really have anything else in mind. Being a third generation insurance agent was of little interest to me and my father graciously accepted that. Perhaps time away would change my mind.

So, as a graduation present, my parents decided to take me to the far away big city and expose me to a real Broadway stage production. That's how, as fate sometimes seems to arrange events, we happened to be at dinner at Mama Minestrone's Restaurant Roma before going to the show we planned to see. The restaurant was one we had picked out of the tourist guide stuff in our hotel room. It was supposed to capture the charm and ambiance of one of the many cultures found around the Big Apple. I was still not quite in synch with the pace and strangeness of the local lifestyle but was managing to cope with obnoxious cab drivers and crowded littered streets. We had enjoyed food somewhat richer and spicier than available back home and were nearing the time to pay the check and leave for the theater when I excused myself to find the men's room. Dad was reviewing the bill, pen in hand, and probably considering what the same fare would have cost back home if it ever replaced beef and potatoes. Mother was wondering if we should take a cab to the theater and risk under tipping another cabdriver.

Those were the last things I remember seeing them do or say. I had found the men's room, taken care of my business, rinsed my hands and was headed back down the hall to the dining area when I heard the first shot that introduced a volley of gunfire. The sound was deafening as it echoed around the dining area. It sounded like a bad B movie scene. I stopped in mid-stride and looked past a wooden screen that separated the dining area from the rear service areas. Two men wearing ski masks had just thoroughly shot a diner and his friends at a table near where we had just dined. So much for our whispered comments about whether the group might be part of the New York lifestyle portrayed in Hollywood movies. Apparently one of the two shooters unintentionally had his weapon on automatic and took out the entire dinner party along with my parents rather than just the host of the other party. My folks were on the floor covered in blood and had died instantly. Our dinner check was still on the table with money to pay it with. Our waiter was among the victims of the massacre. Time seemed to have stopped along with the gunfire.

I watched in horror as the two hoods headed for the front door of the restaurant. I could see a large black sedan parked in the passenger loading zone in front with a driver at the wheel. Apparently the plan was that the massacre would be done quickly and the shooters would be leaving in a hurry. As they were finishing their bloody work and headed toward the entrance, they saw a meter maid, apparently oblivious to the sound of the gunfire, telling their driver to move on. Not wanting to exit carrying freshly fired guns, they turned and headed toward the hall that I was in.

As the shock waves radiating from the bloody scene hit me, I could see that there was nothing I could do to help my parents, except perhaps get myself shot also. Without knowing that I had made a decision, I ran. The hallway back to the bathrooms seemed like the quickest and only exit. It was also the direction that the two gunmen were headed for as they tore off their masks. One of them seemed to have a bad knee that caused him to limp. He was headed toward the same hall I was in and was blocking the other guy, who was trying to get around him. That delay gave me a split second of lead time. In a state of absolute panic, I headed for the fire door at the end of the hall and to the left.

My feet seemed to operate in slow motion though I knew that I was running for my life. Finally after what seemed to take hours, I reached the exit. Then, realizing that the shooters would be right behind me, I pushed the door open before retreating back a few steps to the men's room. I had just entered a stall, closed the door, and climbed up on the toilet when the bathroom door crashed open. I heard a voice saying, "He must have gone into the alley." Saved by a commode! I heard the alley exit door slam shut behind them.

By that time the police were arriving and I was able to make my way back to the chaos in the dining room, kneel, and say goodbye to my parents. That's the tragic 'accident' that left me an orphan. My parents were buried in the family plot back home. I have never since been to the town where I spent the first eighteen years of my life. I suppose there are still relatives back there but I could not imagine living there after what had happened. My high school friends suddenly became history, part of another life.

Of course being the only living witness to the massacre who was willing to talk, or not smart enough not to, I was encouraged to testify against the killers. They, being loyal to their family organization, took the fall for the killings. Perhaps there was some acceptance on their part that they might not have been caught if their planning had been better. As they rushed out that back door, it had slammed shut and locked behind them just as they were confronted by the rear of a garbage truck backing down the narrow alley to hook onto a trash container. At least when they had climbed onto the tailgate trying to find a way out of the alley, the driver had the chance to do something he had always dreamed of. He hit the control lever and bagged the fleeing felons as part of the trash he was loading.

So it was heroism for him and hiding for me. I did agree to stand up in court and identify the suspects. That made me a possible target for future gangland retribution. My new friends in the Justice Department decided that I should drop from public view and start a new life. And where better for an eighteen-year-old to go than into the military with lots of similar looking guys around and all of us behind fences most of the time. Within a day after the trial that I testified at, my name was changed, I had a new social security number, family pictures, and a crew cut to go with the initial uniform issue. Seaman Recruit new name was on the far side of the country from New York. After a forever flight across the country, escorted by a guy who made much less conversation then the average Trappist monk, we were met at the San Diego Airport by a young navy officer attorney. His orders were to be sure I was safely behind the fence at the Naval Training Center. You guys know him as Ernie. He was my first friend in my new life. He has never asked questions about why I was delivered to him as a 'package' by a silent guy in a cheap suit so many years ago. I know that he may have wondered though.

The Seaman Recruit title changed as I completed the basic training and spent four years before deciding that it was safe to get out and get on with my life using my new name. Apparently no one was still looking for me and I was comfortable being who I was now. So on to college where your mother met a navy veteran with no family but ready to start one. And we did.

The other part of the story that needs correction is about my work, how I have made a living all these years. Your world was that of a father who went downtown every day to a job shuffling papers at the Federal Building. My world was of a person given a second chance that led to love, a family, and a normal life that many people would think of as boring. It's like surviving a serious accident and gaining a totally different view on life. So, now you know the rest of the story.

SUNSHINE (CONTINUED)

The first few days were difficult. The police contacts I had knew nothing about what was going on. That figures as normal when the feds don't feel like cooperating or have what they consider to be a good reason not to. The Secret Service guys were out in force driving around town racking up miles between coffee breaks without seeming to make any headway. I did learn more about the rental car, who had rented it after it was picked up at the airport, where they had stayed the days before all the ruckus started, even where they were from. Where they were now was the question. Was the film with them or did someone else have it by now? If necessary, I knew that I could call in some subcontractors to get information about the film from them - after I located them.

I took a flight to their hometown, rented a car, and started the search process. It's a big enough city that questions could be asked without concern as long as I didn't alert their kids. I decided to do the 'headhunter' role, as if I represented a company interested in hiring the guy. They were not due back from vacation yet so this seemed safe as long as I didn't cross paths with other hunters. I even managed to meet with a few of their friends and learned all that I could from them. While the kids were out of the house, I checked phone bills, credit card statements, even grocery receipts, to see what they bought and where they shopped. The wife liked a special type of conditioner for her hair. Perhaps she could try to switch brands. And what about prescription medications? Supplies would not last forever and a doctor somewhere would have to approve more if any condition involved was serious.

With the research done, all that I needed to do was to find them so that the game could proceed. One thing for sure was that the Secret Service would also be looking for the couple. That bunch had an interest at least equal to my employer's in finding the couple and the film. When you can't get into the inner sanctum where all is kept secret, try the sources further out. Such as the people in the outer circles that shuffle the paper waves generated in any government agency. Or those who supply special order stuff. They are more likely to chat during breaks about seemingly routine items.

That's how one of our sources confirmed a special rush order for a large number of 'bugs.' And why did a bill show up for rental of a crop duster plane in the same state where the search started? At least this indicated a logical direction the couple might have headed. Yet there was no indication that they had rented a car? How else would they get one to use? I doubted that the man was an experienced car thief and would not want to be in a stolen car anyway.

It seemed time to check with sources in cities along the main route north as to any activity along the way. Nothing surfaced about the feds being overly active but there was a funny story being passed around in Sacramento. A 'bug' had been found on a sheriff's patrol car by some federal agent who simply claimed it without explanation. One aging and very overweight deputy was taking a lot of flack about maybe his wife was trying to keep tabs on him. If it had been an effort to follow the couple, which direction had they gone from there? When you don't know what to do, do something. I decided to take a quantum leap, apply some basic math skills, and hope that it might save a lot of time. I figured the driving time, plus or minus, up to Seattle and caught a flight north. If they made it that far, they were probably tired, less alert, and might have left some traces.

When I landed there, I checked into a motel and started the slow process of checking the other motels near the airport. The ones with phones at the airport stand near the baggage carousel seemed like a logical place to start. That, of course, was based on an unsupported assumption that they might have driven north and left the car in long-term parking. There were only about twenty-five motels with phones to the airport stand for me to check out. Each check involved a shuttle ride or a drive. My story at each stop was that I was looking for a wife who had run off with her lover and left a husband and six kids. He was having problems in shopping, cooking, and trying to operate the washing machine. After two days of effort, only one clerk remembered anything that might fit. He did recall that in his recent memory, one couple had paid cash for a stay that lasted longer than two hours and seemed more married than the ones that usually do that. They came and went on the airport shuttle and had very little luggage. Not that luggage was required to check in. Maybe they were between flights. But where would they head from Seattle? They might not want to risk airport check-ins or trying to cross into Canada. It would be easier and less risky to take a boat to Alaska. I did the private eye looking for errant husband routine at the Alaska Marine Highway Terminal and scored a home run. A couple in unfazed jeans with new backpacks and vests had paid cash for a cabin as last minute walk-ons at a recent sailing headed for Juneau. The flags raised by cash, new gear, and no reservations had been confirmed as valid when someone else had stopped in to inquire about the couple. Maybe it was time to find out if the San Diego police had made any phone calls to this area code and then to fly north to see if my targets were trying to fade into the wilderness of Southeast Alaska.

BONK - THE POKER GAME

There are five of us who try to get together every Wednesday evening for a session of low stakes dealer's choice poker. If a regular can't make it due to work, vacation or wife's objection, we have some guys that will sit in. It's worked pretty well over the years, a boy's night out, a few brews, win or lose a few bucks. We have a cop, a lawyer, a deputy coroner, a real estate wheeler-dealer who has won and lost several shirts in the local up and down market, and the mandatory (for San Diego) retired navy guy. We usually meet in the back room of a burger/joint pool hall out on Midway Drive not too far from our homes on Point Loma.

My mind was not totally on the game on the night that I planned to blind-side Ernie. I coasted along winning a few hands while trying to pick the right moment to spring my surprise on him. We were about two hours into the evening when two of the guys went out front to hustle up some burgers and more brews. The third guy left to make a beer deposit. That left me and Ernie, neither of us knowing what the other knew. I made my gambit by asking him how he liked his new Blazer.

As he was starting to warm up about great mileage and all the bells and whistles, I dropped the bomb. "So how was the mileage on the trip up to Seattle and back down here?" I was expecting him to blink, flinch, anything, but there was not a sign.

He's a great poker player but I didn't expect him to be that good.

Then he smiled and said, "Let me tell you about the couple that kept going to a doctor to see if they were using the right techniques in making love. The third time the doctor checked them out as OK, he asked why they kept coming back when he and his nurse could not see any problem in technique or result. The man looked a bit sheepish and finally said 'We can't go to my house because my wife is home all day. We can't go to her house because her husband would be upset. And if we come here, Blue Cross covers it..' "

"So," I said.

"So," he said, "Let's just say that two people in a loaned car took a trip together and after a thousand miles of 'togetherness' there will be no divorce as a result and Blue Cross won't have to pay any more medical claims for a weekly checkup."

As the others returned with the burgers and brew, we resumed the game. I was no further ahead in my investigation and may have shown him one of my cards. In any event, he was the big winner on the next hand and I lost.

What about Mom?

It's my turn to add something to the journal that your father has been working on ever since we landed up here away from you guys and the life together that we knew. It has not been easy for us. In some ways it is almost like the story of the man without a country, except that we still have one called our family. It's just that we can't participate in it the same way we did before. So much is the same and so much is totally different. We want to be back where we were but, aside from the weird circumstances, have to admit that it is not all bad here. In fact, if you guys were here fishing, hiking, and skiing, it would be just perfect.

Let me start by saying that the various random events that merged to overturn our lives arrived in a very unpretentious way. As things in life often do. Dad and I were thoroughly enjoying the San Diego scene as we took the days one at a time. I was being firm in my resolve not to call you guys everyday about keeping the house neat, bringing in the mail and the newspaper, and being sure to set the trash cans out. Our trip was the first time we had vacationed without you. We were enjoying the chance to become reacquainted outside the role of being parents. It took a good bit of adjustment before we realized that we were the ones who had to talk to each other when we ate out. Being able to go places without having to be sure three others agreed with the choice was a pleasant new experience, though we kept talking about what the boys would enjoy there in San Diego.

On that last calm morning in San Diego, we had slept in as late as parents ever do even on vacation. At least it was later than usual when we finally emerged into a day of bright sunshine and blue skies. We had stopped by the motel office to check some directions to one of the missions that we wanted to see. The lady at the front desk suggested that if we drove up past the mission in Presidio Park, we might want to have breakfast at a small place up in the Hillcrest area. As Dad was headed that direction, I got busy putting away folders and stuff that had accumulated from our wandering. That's when I found a roll of film in a black plastic canister in the glove compartment. Dad assured me that it was not a roll that he had placed in there, so we decided that it had been left by an earlier renter of the car. We would turn it in later with the car.

We enjoyed a truly fabulous breakfast at the small bakery/café up in Hillcrest. Sitting at a sunlit table in front of the café, we listened to the locals chatting over coffee and watching life go by at a leisurely pace. After we reluctantly pried ourselves away from the place, we spent some time driving around in the area looking at the older homes and manicured lawns in that long established and quieter part of San Diego. Life around there seemed to be ignoring the hustle down Washington to Pacific Highway and I-5 or through the park to the Mission Valley motels and malls. We had a light late lunch at a nice place in La Jolla after dropping off several rolls of film at a place out on Midway Drive. Then we headed back to the motel for resting and reading by the pool before finally thinking about where we would have dinner. On the way we stopped to see if our pictures were ready. I wanted to send some prints to you guys so that you could share in our fun. And a note to remind you about some chores.

I waited in the car while Dad went in the shop to pick the prints up. In less that a minute he came back out really hurrying and looking like he had lost his new tan. He is usually so calm and in control, but now he seemed dazed, shaken up, not fully in control. He got behind the wheel, fumbled the key into the ignition, and almost drove us into a carryall parked near us. I asked if the prints were ready but didn't get an answer. He rushed out of the parking lot narrowly missing a police car that was entering it. Somehow he got us a mile or so down the road through the traffic lights and into another parking lot on Rosecrans. He opened his door, leaned out, and threw up. Most of the debris landed on the pavement rather than on him or the car. The driving and the throwing up are not your dad's usual style, as you well know. I handed him a tissue to help clear off the residue. After that, we walked to a burger place at the far end of the lot. I got us cold drinks while he finished cleaning up in the men's room.

When we were both seated and he was finally starting to tell me what had hit him and was mentioning something about a body, I looked past him to where our rental car was sitting next to the mess on the pavement. Police cars now surrounded the rental car and two officers were approaching it with drawn guns. My first thought was that they must really frown on public barfing around here. Then I noticed that a canine unit was being unloaded. I said "Let's go." and Dad got up and followed me out the front door where a city bus had just pulled up. We got on and I dropped the fare in the box for us as we headed for seats near the rear exit. I remember the bus crossing the railroad tracks just past Pacific Highway and signals for an oncoming train clanging just after we crossed. In a few more blocks we passed our motel, got off at the next stop, and walked back to our room.

Dad still was not talking much, but turned the TV on. There, under a banner of 'Breaking News' was our rental car surrounded by police. Lab technicians were taking samples of the mess Dad had left. The canine unit was sniffing around the burger place. Other news choppers were hovering overhead. There was talk about a murder at a photo shop on Midway Drive and 'people of interest' wanted for questioning. Dad muttered something about "Bad timing on my part to walk in on that scene. Sorry I panicked. Let's pack."

Thinking back, I should have wondered why he didn't just call the police, why he didn't..., why...?

We quickly changed clothes and stuffed what we could from our suitcases into our daypacks. The rest of our stuff was still in our room as we left the motel, tried to casually cross the street, and headed for the Old Town area. The next few hours were a haze of shuttles, trolley rides, and finally finding ourselves in a home above the water out near Ocean Beach. Just when I was starting to feel like the roller coaster was slowing down to let us off as Ernie talked, Dad suggested that he and I take a walk out onto the deck.

What he told me as we stood there in the darkness left me stunned and reeling. Now it was my turn to be shaken to the core of my being.

Nothing that I had ever imagined could compare to the feelings that raced through me as he told his reason for running. I now know to some extent what wives go through when a husband, the father of their joint children, comes out of the closet. If we were not so joined at the hip, I could not have almost calmly decided to ride this situation out with him. What choice was there? Love for him in this, our plight, wanting for you kids to be safe. I had to make a decision beyond making.

Anyway, you heard many times how I met your dad when he was a junior and working on the college daily. He interviewed me about teaching as a career. Actually it was sort of a setup, as I had seen him around the campus and liked his looks, apparent calmness, and a degree of calm maturity beyond the guys a bit younger than him. It was easy enough to have a girl friend also in the journalism school suggest an interview for a series that was being done on careers. A girl needs a way to meet a guy without carrying a sign. Anyway, it worked, we worked. We have had a better marriage and better kids than would ever have seemed possible.

But never did I ever dream or imagine that his pre-college life was what it was. He didn't talk about how his parents had died except to say that it was a tragic accident, that he joined the navy as a way of moving on from the tragedy, and then entered college. Our life together never gave any hint that he had lived the events he had so many years before. He never talked of high school days or friends back then. The only hint of a past was his navy time and our life together. Now, in retrospect, I remember that he never liked to watch movies like The Godfather, had no desire to ever travel to the East

Coast and preferred to be in the background in public activities. I always attributed that to his being modest. He also never had any interest in hunting even when you boys passed through the gun phase.

If a spouse or a child dies, tragically or otherwise, you try to deal with it, well or poorly, go through the grief thing, and somehow move on. He had moved on all those years back, but yet perhaps never fully grieved. Now my choice was to move on, not from a physical death, but because of something that had happened to him over twenty years ago and something else that had happened to us today. But these circumstances carried the hope of ultimately, sooner or later, returning to a new version of our prior life.

Maybe the detour would be short while Dad and Ernie figured out some way to solve it. If not for the potential danger to all of us if Dad's past became our present, no way would I have made the choice that I did. I had to decide in a few minutes what I never would have wanted to decide and had to do it without days to think it over. But decide I did and off we went. Our life and his prior life were now separate chapters blending into our future together.

So go I did, we did. The options at that point seemed to be slim or none. We have been married long enough and are comfortable enough together to survive almost forty hours confined in a mid-sized vehicle over the seemingly endless miles between San Diego and Seattle. The scenery ranged from urban sprawl of houses and beaches to the urban sprawl of houses and trees. Mostly it was car and trucks coming toward us or passing us at speeds we felt would lead to disaster. We became intimately familiar with the front seats of the Blazer to the point of knowing almost by name every crease in the seats.

After Los Angeles, traffic lightened up a bit or perhaps was just spread out more and moving faster. The Central Valley was a blur of high-speed traffic, which thickened up again when we reached Sacramento. By that time we realized someone was trying to keep in touch with us, so we ended that threat easily and moved on. Portland came and went with more stop and go traffic and high bridges. Then it was just head for the finish line in Seattle where we could leave the Blazer for someone else to sit in all the way back to San Diego.

I suppose that under more pleasant circumstances, I would have enjoyed some of the scenery along the way, but my mind was not on sightseeing. Life was reduced to essentials: drive, eat, potty time, nap, drive some more. The motel in Seattle was a room with no view except the back of another motel, a haven to rest in, regroup our energy, and move on from. Maybe after all the sudden change in our lives, the openness and friendliness of where we are now seems to promise that even with the uncertainty, all will be OK.

Maybe part of it is also that Dad's secret life is finally part of our life together. Our having to leave our mutual past together made me understand what he had gone through by himself.

SUNSHINE - WELCOME TO ALASKA

When I first arrived in Juneau, I didn't expect to be there for very long. After all how long should it take to locate two people traveling together in a town of less than thirty thousand people you can't drive away from? The whole place population wise didn't cover the distance between some freeway exits back home. The two would probably stick out like ripe tomato on a peanut butter and jelly sandwich. The flight north from Seattle took less than three hours including a stop at one airport where the taxiway to the terminal was downhill and around a curve. My travels have taken me to a lot of airports around the world but that one and the final approach into Juneau are different to say the least.

The immediate plan was to make a quick check of the area, locate the couple, retrieve the film and quickly conclude this assignment one way or another so that I could get to something more challenging. What this involved and to what extent depended to a large part on the couple. I couldn't just walk up to them, say "I believe that you have some film that you found in San Diego," have them give me the film, and everything would be finished. For one thing, I don't use such a direct approach. For another, face to face is not my style; public recognition I can do without. I knew they didn't run this far just to give up something they could have gotten rid of two thousand miles further south.

As I got to the end of the jet way and headed for baggage claim, the chatter of the passengers being greeted and the greeters seemed unlike any airport I had ever been in. Everybody seemed to know almost everybody else. Almost like a family reunion, with me being the only one who didn't know somebody. When I finally got my bag off the belt and headed for the cab line to get over to the Best Western where I had booked a room, the driver even suggested that I split a fare with some folks headed out into the valley. That doesn't happen where I come from.

The reality of my search possibilities hit home the next morning after breakfast when I walked a few blocks over to the Nugget Mall to pick up some local clothes and rain gear, along with a good map of the area. According to the stuff I found at a travel agency, the city and borough used to be the largest city in the United States in area, though now Long Beach is bigger. Yet only about thirty thousand people live in the borough. Most of the work and business and living is done within an eight to ten mile radius of the older original downtown area, which would seem to make a search easier. Some families that don't mind icy roads and the occasional deer on the road live further out Glacier Highway or out north on Douglas Island, but most seem to like being closer in.

The other local lore that I picked up as I wandered and talked was that nearly everyone here seems to work in city, state, or federal jobs or something related to them or supporting them or are retired from them. Tourism is big business during the summer months. The fishing, logging, and mining jobs are still alive locally, but not to the extent they once were. Aside from all that, according to a city survey, when the locals are not at work the number one recreational activity, even ahead of fishing, is hiking. Watching TV is down at ten on the survey. Sex was apparently not on the survey list, though I assumed it does take place.

From this early looking around I gathered that most people, including the ones I was looking for, would probably not be found hanging around the business areas, except maybe at the local Fred Meyer or Costco stores when shopping. If they were mall types, the Nugget Mall might be the place to go looking. Yet how much time could even a dedicated mall fan spend there? It's not like Mall Of The Americas in Minnesota or Mission Valley in San Diego. If I wanted to, I could wait for the big local events like the Folk Festival or July 4th parade where the whole town shows up.

Where all of this left me was probably having to check the ninety or more local trails one at a time or drive up and down Egan Drive or Glacier Highway hoping they would pop up. Or maybe I could hang out at the Nugget Mall or Fred Meyer or Costco with the same hope. Everything so far was pure chance. I didn't think that I could or wanted to go door to door looking for them.

I also quickly realized that another hurdle to looking for them here is that the people here are quite different from the other places that I have been. It seemed like a really nice place with great people who are open to new people in town which makes newcomers locals very quickly.

The people here are even friendly to the tourists who show up in droves during the season and whose numbers made it even harder for me to search. It would be easier after the tourist season was over in a few months. For now, it was great to search while surrounded by snow-capped glaciers and the green-forested slopes so different from where I have always lived.

While I looked around and thought about all the places the couple might be and how long it might take to find them, I needed a place to live while I searched. It would have to be a place where I could come and go at any time of the day or night without making any neighbors wonder about my erratic schedule. Most apartment complexes would be out because light sleepers could be disturbed and complain to a spouse, other live-in, or co-worker, thereby drawing attention to me. The place also needed to have quick and easy access to all parts of the city from the Valley to downtown and over to Douglas Island. Juneau, according to my map, had one main route to drive in and out of town by way of Egan Drive. You can take Willoughby and Glacier Avenue part way and then you need to get back on Egan Drive. For those wanting a scenic or slower route Glacier Highway starts again after the Salmon Creek intersection and winds through the Lemon Creek area. As most people would use Egan Drive, a good place to watch people go by would be someplace like a room at the Breakwater Motel overlooking the drive and the harbor. Renting a room there long-term would use up a lot of the per diem I was being paid and also draw too much attention.

I had thought about all these points while having breakfast at the Breakwater one morning. If I had spent less time thinking about operational details, I might have paid more attention to the couple at the next table and realized that they were a perfect match for the profile of the couple that I was looking for. What a coincidence that would have been. But I continued my thinking about location, location, location as I left the motel and returned to my rental car where I had parked on the nearby street. Next to the Breakwater was a small two-story house facing Glacier Avenue with the back near Egan Drive. A "For Rent" sign was in the front window. I copied the number, later called the owner at a Seattle area number, and arranged to view and rent the place. Now I could watch coming and going traffic if and when I needed to and could come and go without neighbors paying attention. They would assume that it was motel traffic and I would have my privacy.

My next concern was how to pass the time while not searching. That is one way that this work is like being in a hospital; you can only read so many books and magazines or take more than a day of television. Hanging out in bars is an option but 'Smoke Gets In Your Eyes' has never been my favorite song. Being basically a city guy, all the outdoor space around me was hard to adjust to. I am used to a neighborhood with stores and movies, places to walk to, wall-to-wall people. Exercise is something you do in a gym and a walk is something you do on a Sunday in a park with the wife and kids. Walking, called hiking here, in a virtual wilderness would be a challenge with no bathrooms, no traffic noise, no park police, and with some hikers packing guns. This would take some getting used to. Those long ago Boy Scout days were nothing like what I was faced with here. Reluctantly, I shopped for instruction books and trail guides and outdoor gear and started out.

All of this put me, unexpectedly, in a sort of mid -life crisis. My current career path had leveled off; targets that really needed or deserved dispatching were now, as a result of my skills, fewer in number. I was also starting to miss the day-to-day aspects of the work I had done before my retirement. Friendships and coffee sharing were not part of this job. Yet I had a job to do and tried to concentrate on my work. So I began to think through what I knew, what I was faced with, and what I could do to resolve the conundrums. I realized now that short of a chance encounter, a lot of time and waiting might be involved in finding the couple. There were just too many places they could be that I was not at when they were. Maybe I needed to stop looking locally and think more globally. For now, with winter coming on, the places to watch and search might cover less ground area, but with a different set of conditions. Time to come in from the cold and think more.

I began to consider why a couple, even under their circumstances or because of them, would just drop out as they did. A husband in an imagined or real mid-life crisis might be tempted to leave a boring job, be lured away by a younger woman not yet nicely aged, or just be infected by the 'is this all there is' virus. But a woman, apparently happily married with kids in college and enmeshed in their lives would be a different matter. I could not even imagine what would ever convince my wife to take such a step unless maybe she found out what my consulting work really involved.

Perhaps there was something in his or her history, something that might or might not be a major factor in finding them or the film, but might lead to other history that caused them to run. Maybe he was really a fugitive financier or the real life Fugitive like on TV. More and deeper hometown research seemed to be needed. From my trip back there I knew a lot about them. I knew ages, education, military service as shown on his DD 214, place of employment, type of car, and that his parents were not living. I could almost write a resume for him or her. Their birth certificates checked out all right. Maybe everything was too much in order.

That's when it finally sunk in that this was not the usual locate, figure routines, draw up an action plan, and work the plan situation. The quarry is usually more visible, highly aware, and well protected. While a target may try to stay out of view, that is very difficult for a public figure, whether rock star, politician, drug lord, or head of state. They have to come and go, appear in public, and lead lives that always give an opening of some sort for people in my line of work.

This assignment presented some interesting challenges that were not usually present. The pair were not public figures needing to appear to speak, perform or conduct business. If they had food, water, and shelter, they could stay out of sight indefinitely. Sure, they would have to buy groceries, maybe see a doctor or dentist, or react to cabin fever. Otherwise, they could blend in with the trees and rain. If and when they did go from place to place, there would be a chance of seeing them. I did realize early on that one thing done here and one way to combat cabin fever would be to be outdoors. Except that the 4,200 square miles of local outdoors made a lot of places to be somewhere in.

If they were found, the next question would be whether they had the film with them, had left it with someone, or left it in some place outside Alaska. If I acted, what might that trigger?

Whatever was on the film could not be used for leverage if it became public knowledge. And the use of violence to learn the film location violated my feelings about violence. It is not so much an objection to death as to how it is arrived at.

THE LAST FRONTIER

My instructions from the agent in charge of the San Diego fiasco were to pack to stay warm and dry, and to expect the assignment to last as long as it took to locate and retrieve or destroy the film, if it had not been developed. I was also to be sure that the couple was not aware of what was on the film or of its importance. If it had been developed, all known prints were to be destroyed and steps taken to prevent any others from ever being found. Before I headed for REI and other outdoor equipment stores to gear up for my expedition, I did raise some points that I thought might get me off the hook. Like, why not just send them a letter at their home address and tell them to return the roll of film? I mean, why not take advantage of the fear factor generated when an unexpected letter arrives from the government?

The agent sending me off to the distant wilderness far from known civilization looked at me and said, "Aside from the fact that what we would be asking them to return is not government property, such a simple request would raise more questions. Such as why we want it. It would indicate that we, the almighty federal government, have an interest in it. That, in turn, leads to wondering why we are interested in it. If we don't show an interest, then we are not interested and if questioned can say that we are not interested. Therefore nothing happened to cause us to be interested. And no roll of film exists that we are interested in."

His circular logic seemed par for the way Washington and government does things.

One minor concern I had as a result of the 'logic' was that there could be no revealing in any way that I was assigned to and working for the Secret Service. That meant that I could not work with local or state police agencies. Which very much tied my hands - and feet - as I headed for an area known for having a lot of ice and snow. I was deprived of a lot of potential resources that could have made my work easier.

The other minor problem was that my prior work with my home agency had been almost all deskwork, mostly overseas, analyzing information collected by others on the front lines of intelligence gathering. I had never done actual fieldwork since my basic agency training days. To say that I was in over my head on this assignment would be an understatement. But orders being exactly that, I smiled and went.

So my job was to go to a place where I didn't know anyone and find a guy and his wife without knowing how to do something like that. I had seen the guy from the back as he went into the photo shop in San Diego, seen him from the front as he hurried out bent over trying not to throw up, and sort of from the side as he finally did it. Not much to go on. The wife was in the car while all this was going on and not really visible. There were grainy surveillance photos from SEATAC airport, but those were like the ones on the late news showing the local convenience store robber - grainy and not very helpful. I didn't even have a wife to listen to my gripes about all of this, even if I could tell anyone.

My first hint of things to come was at the boarding area in the Seattle airport. As the crowd waited for the boarding call, lots of them were talking to other passengers headed home about what they had been doing 'outside.' Then, when I arrived at the Juneau Airport, I began to feel like a wallflower at the big dance. Nearly everybody seemed to know everyone around the baggage claim area as I was waiting for my bags, which finally showed up after the happy crowd had headed off in cars, trucks, and shuttle vans.

This was not a good introduction to a place where I might be for a few months or even years if the job took that long. Finally I took a cab to the nearest motel, which was all of two minutes and one stop sign away from the airport, and checked in. I had a lonely dinner in the restaurant and wondered if I had arrived at the end of the world or somewhere beyond. When I paid my check, I did make a casual inquiry about whether nightlife existed in the Juneau area. The waiter laughed and said, "Welcome to Juneau. Aside from places like this and what folks do at home, this is pretty much it. There is the street scene downtown, legislators and tourists in season doing the scene at the Baranoff, and for the rest of us, maybe the Sandbar. For that, you had better like Western."

The next morning I rented a car and started to explore my place of exile. I could imagine how Napoleon felt on Elba. A local map came with the rental, but was of little use. You go mainly north or south till the main road ends or cross the bridge from town and go north or south again till the road ends. From the ends of the roads, it looked like walking or boating would be the way to go. I managed to tour all of the main roads in a little over two hours. Then I spent some time driving around the residential area near the glacier in the Valley and up and down the hills above the downtown area. In less than half a day, I almost knew my way around the area.

While I was driving and then walking around downtown and then in the stores in the valley, I felt very overdressed for the party. Sure, some of the people around the state and federal buildings were shirt and tie types, but the average garb was more faded jeans or Carhartt work wear. Flannel shirts must have been invented here, or at least sold very well. The most unusual sight to me, though, was the number of carefully groomed women headed into the state and federal buildings, not in heels or flats, but instead tennis shoes or rubber boots or hiking boots. I assumed that they had more stylish dress shoes in their work area to slip on during the day. Maybe my water soaked loafers would have to be replaced with something to fit local walking conditions.

My next stop after the tour I had taken was out to the Nugget Mall in the valley area to load up on jeans, flannel shirts, good rubber boots and hiking boots, a parka with liner, and all the related stuff to cope with the local weather and terrain. I was starting to fit in clothes-wise, but it would take a few rounds of washing to get the newness out of the stuff.

Then I rented a small one bedroom apartment out in the valley on Lori Avenue not far from the Mendenhall Mall where I could hole up when not looking for the couple. An investment of six hundred dollars of my expense money bought me a small car with a good engine and tires surrounded by terminal rust. Now I was ready to start my search, assuming that the couple was actually here. Again, government logic. The fact that you have not found them does not mean they are not here, just that you have not found them. Until you are sure they are not here because they have been found someplace else, keep looking because they still might be where you are. Besides, where else would you look? If they have not been found here or someplace else, looking here is just as productive as looking someplace else. Keep looking.

That evening, after another solitary meal at a place called The Broiler in the Nugget Mall where everyone else seemed to be having fun, I drove back into downtown. Apparently most of the tourists had retreated to their cruise ships for dinner and bingo, or headed by bus to the Salmon Bake, so the streets were less crowded than earlier. Outside the downtown bars, The Rendezvous, The Triangle, and the Imperial Billiard and Bar, small knots of people stood listlessly smoking and chatting. I wondered, if this was the type of people found outside, what would it be like inside? They didn't seem like warm and fuzzy types who would welcome someone like me into their space. I headed back for the Valley and circled the streets around the Nugget Mall until I found the Sandbar. Many of the cars and pickups parked outside had certainly seen better times. No shiny new Cads or Mercedes were to be seen in these parts. I parked and headed for the entrance. As I walked in, I was hit twice: once by the haze of exiting smoke and once by the blast of music. The music was definitely vintage Western delivered at maximum loud with maximum twang by a group of five musician wannabes on a rickety stage near the entrance. Nondescript would have been a kind way to describe their jeans, facial hair, and Western style shirts on two of the group. Nashville it was not, but the scene conjured up images of every 'why my love left me in a pickup truck headed for jail stuck on the railroad track' song ever written. The lights were low, the beer signs were flashing, and the place was packed even though it was early evening on a weeknight.   What would a weekend night bring besides the police? I headed back to my car and my lonely but quiet apartment and thought about how to get on with my mission.   Better that than secondhand smoke and ruptured eardrums.

As analysis of raw data is my normal work, that's where I then started.   Back to the basics.   If the couple is here, they must be living together. They most likely would be renting, not buying or camping out.   Renting would be most likely, as no public records would be kept. That way, there would be no record of a house purchase or a loan application.

They would need money to live on, which would have to be earned or brought along or sent to them somehow.

They would have to buy food.   There were only four main places to do that.

They might seek medical or dental help - along with a lot of other people. Or they might not, if they didn't need any such help.

They might buy a car, might get driver's licenses, or might do a lot of things. Without help from police and state agencies, I could not get access to sources that could get me information in those areas. The regional or home office might be able to tap such records, but again, that might raise questions.

I could inquire casually at some places about locating recent arrivals who were old friends that I was trying to get in touch with. Unless carefully done, that might blow my cover or even get back to the people I needed to find. Or I could shop a lot, hoping to spot them at the Mall or at a grocery store or some other store. The difficulty with that is that we as protectors were trained to screen out ordinary people like these were while looking for hints of who might be a bubble off center and a likely threat to the people we were guarding. As these people were 'normal', I probably wouldn't see them anyway.

I also needed what the pros call a cover story, something that I could be seen doing at various places without having to answer a lot of questions. As this area has a long mining history and reeks of ruins of those by-gone days, maybe I could be compiling a photo essay about those times and places. That would get me out and around a variety of places where I could pretend to poke around and maybe watch people go by. While I had been driving around earlier in the day, I had found Savikko Park south of Douglas in West Juneau and wandered around the area near the picnic shelter. A path there turned into a trail that lead to a junction with what my tourist map said was the Treadwell Mining Area. I looked at the buildings and the rusting metal everywhere and knew that I had found my cover and maybe a hobby. At least I wouldn't have to spend my time at the Sandbar on weeknights.

Another factor I considered as I made my decision was that someone else had to be looking for them also. The scenes on the film would be of real value to someone or some group wanting to embarrass or leverage the administration. I had to believe that at least one other person or group of persons was in the area also looking for the couple. They might have more backing than I had and be willing to go to lengths that I could not. I hoped that my cover would be good enough to protect me. Off we go into the wild green and wet yonder.....

THE LAST RESORT

After about a month of hiking the more used and better maintained trails, we decided that it was time to try to locate the shelters just in case we needed a place to run to. Our goal was to look for and at them to see whether they might fit that ultimate need if and when it came along. There was also a mutual feeling that we needed to break away from the known to the unknown to see how we handled it.

By that time, we had hiked enough of the trails in the area and talked to enough other hikers to know some of the basic trail mantras. Carry a backpack with survival gear: water, food, first aid stuff, rain gear, dry socks, and so forth. Be ready to stay out overnight even if you don't plan to. Don't leave the main trail and go off cross-country unless you intend to get lost. You can leave a paved road or a street in a housing area and be turned around in a wilderness situation in less than a hundred feet. When that happens, stop, don't panic, look around. Most times you can follow your muddy steps back to where you started from.

Also, be aware of the bears. They live here also and sometimes can be on the same trail or road. Don't try to pet them.

Expect weather changes. Carry a map and a compass and be able to use them. Don't drink the water unless you enjoy diarrhea, also known as beaver fever. And the basic rule we had to ignore because of our situation: Let someone know where you are going and when you expect to be back.

This hike, then, would be our first challenge to see if we could go off on our own and come back safely. It would be to a more remote and primitive area than what our daily hikes took us to. If we got into trouble, there would be very little chance of other hikers coming along to bail us out. With these encouraging thoughts, we drove out Thane Road past the avalanche zone to the trailhead, checked our socks and boots for comfort, donned our packs, and headed up the trail.

The first part of the trek was the usual steady uphill climb followed by more up around switchbacks. So far, nothing remarkable except the distant sound of rushing water. At the top of the climb, we looked out over a vivid green valley that seemed to stretch for miles. The trail down into the valley was almost invisible. After we descended, we found that the path along the valley floor paralleled Sheep Creek much of the time. It was easy to imagine miners seeking gold where we were hiking. When we reached the far side of the valley and started up, we got back to reality in a hurry. This part of the trail obviously didn't get much attention from the trail maintenance people.

We pushed slowly through the dense underbrush that almost completely covered the trail. Some parts of the path had eroded away and left only thin air to walk on if not watchful. We pushed our way onward and upward, wondering whether there might ever really be an end to the battle. Finally, after almost an hour of struggle, we reached the tree line and were in open meadows. It was a welcome relief, even though we realized that we would be returning the same way. We knew that such a difficult ascent would keep a lot of less dedicated hikers away if we ever had to stay up here.

The shelters, when we reached them, were just that, nothing more, nothing fancy. Culvert pipe, regardless of size, lacks style. It was just a place to hunker down if weather turned sour, a place where bears couldn't easily intrude even if they could bang on the outside. And definitely not posh country living, only a place to hide if necessary at some times of the year. We hiked back down after nicknaming the place 'The Last Resort.'

Becoming Part Of The Woodwork

During our first summer here, Mom and I learned a lot about the more down-to-earth aspects of the local trail system by studying the local trail guides, hiking with local hikers, and also by volunteering to do trail upkeep after we saw a notice in the Juneau Empire. The group seeking trail brushing help was started by local trail users because the city, state, and federal agencies responsible for the trails never seemed to have enough funds to do upkeep over the multitude of trails that are always at the mercy of weather, heavy use, and old age. The rampant growing season, starting with early sighting of skunk cabbage, followed by towering tangles of Devil's Club, quickly covers the trails with brush. Frequent heavy rain washes away the trail surfaces. Hikers taking shortcuts do further damage. Many of the trails dated back to when the natives used them for fishing and hunting pathways before they became wider trails during the mining and logging era. Now the trails are paths for hikers, mountain bikers, runners and the occasional bear. Not to mention an occasional horse or all terrain vehicle rider on some trails.

Local trail guides answered a lot of our questions about the ups and downs and history of the system. The Forest Service guide was extremely helpful, as was the one written by a local author named Mary Lou King. She and her husband have apparently spent a lot of time on the local trails and know them as well as anyone. We had picked up copies at the Forest Service counter in Centennial Hall shortly after getting here. The most important thing we learned from the books and the trail group was to always take survival gear and be ready to camp if you get lost. Getting confused or lost is very easy to do if you leave the trail you are hiking on to go off exploring. There are many local stories about hunters and hikers who learned this lesson by spending cold, wet days hoping to be rescued and dreaming of a pizza at Bullwinkle's.

Most Saturdays we joined the Juneau Parks and Recreation Saturday Hike group to get further acquainted with the trails and the people of our new town. There is a Wednesday group and a Saturday group that each have different personalities. A volunteer leader would meet the group of the day, regulars and novices, at the designated trailhead. After howdies, gossip, and signing in, the group would take off up or down the trail. The regulars always seemed well prepared, while tourists and newcomers sometimes failed to bring essentials like hats and rain gear. Most times we would have a lunch break at the end of the trail and then hike back by the same route, unless we happened to be on one of the few loop trails around here.

When fall approached, the last cruise ship departed as the mountaintops started to show white, which the locals call 'termination dust.' We arranged to house-sit another place further out the road and even more off the beaten track and harder to get to in winter. It was down a side road, way out Glacier Highway where the trail to the Boy Scout Camp starts. The owner was a commercial fisherperson heading south for the winter. It came with the use of an aging Subaru wagon and a vintage Ford pickup equipped with a plow to use in clearing a path out to the main road when a smaller vehicle would bog down. The truck was stopped by lowering the plow as the brakes were AWOL. Again, there was a dog to feed and firewood to be carried in to heat with. Though the place was a much longer drive from town, it was even more private than our last place. It came with a nice collection of books to read, videos to watch, and music to listen to. There were even sets of cross-country skis we could use to learn on.

Now it seemed like time to come in from the cold that would soon be descending on us and making trail use more difficult. Cross country skiing and snowshoeing looked like the next things to learn to be able to use the trails during the winter months. And as the situation causing us to be here did not appear to be resolved, I took the next step toward hiding in plain sight and went job hunting.

After doing a computer search at the library branch at the Mendenhall Mall to find what might be open at the State, I applied for an entry-level job that seemed to open from time to time and would not require me to answer too many questions. With my new beard, longer hair and not dressing beyond the job, I was able to fill a vacancy in the mailroom in the State Office Building, or 'SOB' in local lingo. Read, sort, follow directions and push the cart on and off the elevator and around the route twice a day. The hardest part was learning how the SOB is laid out.

Because, just in case you ever need to know, there is an old SOB and a new SOB. The old one is on Main Street kitty-corner from the State Capitol and is eight stories high. The back of the old SOB is across a parking lot from the back of the new SOB which is eleven stories high and fronts on Willoughby Street. You enter the new SOB at level two as level one is parking for visitors and executives. The front elevators only go to level eight which is an atrium and a deck looking toward the harbor. The stairs from level one go on to the top floor or you walk through the atrium past the State Library to more elevators that go on up, or down to seven and six. Seven leads to the parking lot between the two SOBs where bears sometimes raid the dumpsters at night. Level eight in the new SOB goes over a sky bridge to level four of the old SOB where you take stairs or elevators down to level two or one for the various exits from that SOB. There are also certain levels to exit or enter the new SOB parking structure depending on when you get to work and try to find a spot. By the time you figure out the various level's routes, you are just about out of the ninety-day probationary period.

The money that I was now bringing in, less retirement, less taxes, less this and that, went automatically into our local account and covered our basic living expenses here. My new union had opted out of Social Security so nothing went there. We did worry a little about maybe having to file a tax return under the names of the deceased couple we now were, but would face that later.

Of course, once you are in the state system and become a face in the crowd on breaks at the snack bar on level eight, you are sort of vetted for other jobs that might come up without having to worry about a long interview process and a lot of reference checks. After I was on permanent status, I started to look around and to chat more often with some of the people I met on my daily rounds. The beard was trimmed and the hair shorter and my overall appearance was neater, which helped me land a clerical job in Administration, and before long, step by step, a contract review job. After almost three years here, I was making the same amount as when we left on our vacation.

Mom didn't want to stay at our home-of-the-month club alone, so she signed on as a volunteer at the main library in downtown next to the wharf where the cruise ships tie up. She rose from volunteer to half-time to full-time in less than a year. It's a good life, except for watching our backs and missing our family. When the president is a lame duck, maybe the pressure will be less. We hike after work most days and on the weekends. We continue to miss our family while we wait to know when the heat is off. Though everything seems to be normal, there are occasional signs that maybe that is too good to be true.

OH BOY(S)

The one letter that came from Mom and Dad and the one phone call from Ernie (was one phone call all that they were allowed; why not one each, and it was not even from them) put us in that situation where you are waiting on hold for the 'next available representative' to come on line. The music, not of your choice or style, plays on and on interrupted only by an artificial voice thanking you for your patience and "please continue to hold." Except that Chris and I didn't have the music or the voice while we were on the never-ending hold. We had a hard time exercising patience. It wasn't so much missing their presence and the things we did as a family, like enjoying mom's cooking, as knowing they were 'out there' somewhere where we couldn't reach them. That made it seem like an ongoing dream that never has an ending.

Here we were, like two oversize bumps on a log, waiting for the next shoe or shoes to fall. We, me and Chris, had taken Mom and Dad to the airport a week or so before all this waiting started. We had expected them back in a month. Jerry, our older brother, who always tried to rein us in, make us sort of legal in a sense, was off doing his military time to help finance his college plans, so he has been mostly out of the loop on all this. Though he does weigh in when he can get here on leave. He thinks we ought to locate them and do our version of a hostage rescue mission. So far we have managed to calm his Rambo tendencies.

Chris and I were in college, me a starting freshman and him a sophomore, when all this stuff started. Our school is not so far from home that we can't get home most weekends or on class breaks. That way, the house gets used, watering done, kept sort of ready for when Mom and Dad get back here, if and when. If the 'hold' ever ends and a voice comes on line.

We were summer vacationing when they left for what was planned to be a month of fun in the sun with no concerns. Our hope was to go and help them with beach duties, such as beach bunny watching, but they said no; it was time for something called 'independent living' for the month. We also wanted to visit with Uncle Ernie who is a more relaxed version of Dad. They go back a long way to ancient times, like over twenty years ago when they were both in the Navy out there.

We were working at our summer jobs while taking some classes and trying not to rack up too many evening miles on the family cars when we got the call from Uncle Ernie. He told us, after a few comments about our batching it, that he had hosted our folks as overnight guests, that everything was pretty much OK, but that there had been some changes in their plans that they had talked about with him. The speaker phone was on as we listened and our first reaction was to wonder what had happened with their motel. Then we wondered why he was calling instead of them. When he said he was calling from a pay phone rather than his home or office, we really began to wonder and have concerns about what was going on.

He told us, "If I tell you what I know and what I think, you might know enough then to be in harm's way. Here's what I suggest as an alternative. You might want to go to the college library or to a newsstand and read the recent issues of the San Diego Union for the past week or so. You will see some local news stories that might answer some of the questions you will have. There is much more that is not reported on because the news hounds have not sniffed it out yet. Maybe they will never connect the dots."

"But your folks are all right, just out of sight while the local air clears. Your mom found something, your dad saw something, and we decided they should continue their vacation, but not around here. There is a letter from them on the way. Be sure that after you get it and read it, you lock it away in a safe place. And don't leave anything around the house that you wouldn't want your minister to find. There may be people visiting when you are not there. Be concerned, but try not to worry. When the dust settles, they will be in touch or I will. Assume that any phone calls you make or get will be recorded, so keep down the heavy breathing with any lady friends."

If not for his calm words with even a trace of humor, we would have been on the next plane west looking for them. But we decided to wait as the days turned into weeks, then months and then years. We went on with our lives of school and work and routines trying not to worry as he had suggested. The house was too quiet at times without Mom and Dad coming and going. And we did on several occasions pick up on little indications that someone had visited us while we were gone. Dust balls here and there were disturbed and neighbors told us about some service trucks parked in the driveway when we hadn't expected anyone. There were also the visits from the San Diego cop and the headhunter who claimed to have a great job opportunity for Dad. What was really going on? Our imaginations ran as wild as teenage males dreaming of San Diego beach bunnies.

We did pour over copies of the San Diego newspaper as Ernie had suggested without reaching any conclusions other than that the whole business was weird. The big news, of course was the national political convention that had been winding up there about the time that Mom and Dad got there. The pictures of the candidate leaving the hotel to return to Washington made him look like something else was on his mind while he was shaking hands with the same person three times. The First Lady looked a bit happier than she usually does; she even was caught smiling in public. With the convention over, the news seemed to shift back to lurid coverage of local crime. The first story, in spite of its tragic nature, had an unusual twist. It was about a photographer killed in a bathroom drowning at the airport. We might not have thought there was anything of interest about that except that a day or two later there was the brutal killing of a clerk at a photo shop. Photo shop equals film which is something photographers use. The police were looking for a witness who fled the scene in a rental car with a woman asking questions. They abandoned a rental car a short distance away. Our imaginations now moved into high gear.

Dad and Mom had been driving a rental car like a lot of tourists do. They could have been at a photo shop, which is a logical place to leave film to be developed. Mom would have wanted to send us pictures to show us the good times they were having. There was a possible link of a dead photographer and a death at a photo shop with a witness being sought. The one other lurid crime about the same time was that of a cross-dresser found dead in a dumpster. That didn't seem to be connected to the other deaths, unless maybe pictures taken by the photographer before his bathroom visit were at the photo shop and somehow had something to do with the cross-dresser. Our imaginations shifted from high gear into overdrive. At this point it seemed like a good idea to be sure Ernie's phone number was out of our family phone listings book even if it seemed like overkill. As agreed we would call him once a month from a different pay phone to his office. The whole thing began to seem like the plot of a low budget spy movie.

If there was some connection between at least two of the three deaths and the folks had somehow witnessed something, why would our folks choose to drop completely out of sight? We would have to wait and see. Certainly there was nothing in his or her life we didn't know about, though some of our escapades were not known to them. When we had a visit by a San Diego police officer a few weeks later, all we learned was that Dad had stumbled onto the photo shop killing and didn't hang around to answer questions. Nothing was said about the other two deaths that we were aware of and we didn't ask.

We were polite with the officer but said we weren't concerned because they were not even due home yet. If we heard from them, we would tell them to contact him. He saw our trophy shelf and talked a bit about football before he left. He also commented on the picture showing Dad way back when he was in the Navy in San Diego.

We told the neighbors and the people who called that Mom and Dad had decided to extend their trip and might even keep going to do some volunteer work.   Before long the questions became less frequent and we came and went and waited.   No news is supposed to be good news, but no news is really just no news. The pace and demands of college and jobs did help some to get us through the waiting. The difficult parts were needing to share some things with them while we moved out into the world on our own.   They, as parents, had done a good job of preparing us for the world we would bump into, but there were still some things we might have learned easier if they had been there to guide us.

Sunshine - The Early Years

Looking back, I don't see that my childhood was anything unusual. My family lived in one of those New Jersey cities across the water from the Big Apple. It had docks, wharves, rundown areas, average small homes along with some where the country club set lived, and lots of commuters. I went to school there, did the little league thing, went to church a while, nothing special in my growing up. Just an average kid, mostly Irish, with good grades, but not expected to ever be on a top ten list in anything. Work, pay your dues, and pass the stick to the next generation.

Dad was on the local police force, a patrol sergeant after only ten years of effort. His dad had been a beat cop too. In New York and New Jersey, there seems to be a strong family pull to fireman or policeman jobs, a tradition of following the elders. Having family ties to use as a foot in the door helps. I tried to go down other paths, but after two years of junior college, I decided that a regular pay check, maybe starting a family, was what I wanted sooner than later. I applied to join the local police force, took the tests, and was accepted as a recruit. After training and surviving my probationary period, I was on my way.

By the time I made my first promotion, I was also promoting the idea of marriage to the girl I had dated off and on since my junior year in high school.

Baby made three, then four, then five. That's when I became a fledgling detective, junior grade. I worked my way up before pulling the plug at twenty years. During my career some local business people had hinted at ways that I could increase my income without changing my tax bracket. My wife also worked as the kids grew. I was not in search of income that could bring us grief in the form of additional bosses. I always made it clear to the guy making any offer that everyone has a job to do - mine to enforce the law and catch bad guys; his to make money by whatever method he choose. If I caught him, I was doing my job. No hard feelings.

That was easy. What was difficult was responding to and investigating the many ways, sick and otherwise, people from every walk of life committed homicides. Guns were only one way they chose to kill each other. Fitted concrete boots, meat hook hangings, snakes, simple suffocation, and pill switching became the litany of my workdays. By the time I hit twenty years on the job, I had seen it all, yet always expected that some new way would show up. At times I pondered about why people didn't figure out some easy and painless way to eliminate the source of a specific irritation or business problem. You don't have to use an assault rifle in a crowded room - unless the intent is to deliver a visual message, like who's in charge of a territory. I thought about this a lot over the years and wondered what might be a better way.

After the gold watch was safely in hand, I launched my business career. I had no formal business plan, no SBA loan, no publicity, just a few succinct words to a few people on the other side of the street I had walked for those twenty years. Like painless dentistry, I would now offer painless dispatching with a minimum of publicity other than an obituary. My years of experience in figuring out unusual ways others had tried and failed helped me in my new career.

Two or three trips a year to exciting new places, all expenses paid, makes my retirement very interesting. My wife is happy that I use my experience to be a consultant on law enforcement matters. How well I am doing? Turn on the TV and watch "Unsolved Crimes"- you won't see any of my assignments featured there. But don't ask me for any trade secrets. You do your job and I do mine.

Which is why this particular assignment intrigued me. Find the people, find the film, and if necessary, quietly dispatch them. Do not leave obvious tracks, like the clowns that killed the people in San Diego. That was murder, not a gentle and painless dispatching.

BONK - TRAVEL TIME

After the poker game effort to rattle Ernie into admitting that he was somehow involved with the witness couple from the photo shop killing, I hit dead ends on all three cases. Apparently the trio that dunked the photographer and were probably responsible for the other two killings left our area with no forwarding address or maybe got retired Hoffa style. The Secret Service guys had finished their 'training' and stopped hanging around San Diego and our shop. The only comment that any of us heard as they left town was one guy grousing about having to buy warm clothes for his next assignment which seemed to be possibly long term.

The only official travel for me was a brief trip back to the mid-west to check out the couple's family. Surprisingly, the two kids at the family home taking summer vacation from college seemed very low key about the fact that their parents had not returned from a vacation trip. Maybe they knew more than they were saying. When I ask them straight out if anyone else had been asking about their parents, they did say that a corporate headhunter had been around trying to contact the father about a job opportunity. That did surprise them because it had never happened before and their father was happy with his job, whatever it was he did at the federal building downtown, and would probably never move from the area.

As a matter of fact, one said, when he did retire, mom and dad had talked about doing some volunteer work to combine with travel. Maybe that was why they were still gone. While we all were talking, I noticed some football trophies over the fireplace and mentioned that I had played college ball. One son was returning to college for his sophomore year and was on the football team, so we hit it off with me relating what my nickname is. As we were looking at pictures on the family room wall, there was a group picture of a training squadron at Naval Training Center-San Diego years earlier. A younger dad was standing in front of a younger Ernie, who was wearing the dress whites of a Navy officer. Bingo, finally. How and when could I play this card?

Before I flew back to San Diego, I did stop by the father's office to see if there had been any word from him. While the staff was cordial, all that I could gather was that all was well and that they would see him when they saw him. He either was a very valued employee or I was not being given all parts of the equation.

The only other travel that I took was unofficial, though I did carry along a snapshot loaned to me by the boys. My wife had been wanting me to take some time off to use up our credit card airline miles. I had been wondering where a logical place would be for people to go from Seattle. Canada is close but the customs agents would have checked people coming and going. The thought of a possible APB might have curtailed that route. What about cruise ships and the Marine Highway System to Alaska?

In order to further promote domestic tranquility, I took a busman's holiday and we flew off to Seattle.

We stayed there a few days, found it to be as crowded as San Diego but wetter and further out to the airport, not like San Diego where you land nearly downtown. We did the Space Needle visit and then the Pike Place Market thing to watch the fish throwers. Things were not that different from some of the tourist things we offer, but maybe a little older. Water and boats and nice but expensive restaurants were not new to us even if my pay didn't get us to them very often. At least we have less rain in San Diego.

While my wife was out exercising our credit cards at various stores to build up more airline miles, I contacted some old friends. They were mainly people who had dropped in on me in San Diego hoping to maybe someday work there. With their help I was able to get access to some airport surveillance videos from around the time the Blazer was there. After several hours of looking, there they were. Dad looked like he had just had a haircut and a shave and Mom sported a new Seahawks sweatshirt. They looked as if they had just driven a thousand miles and were ready to rest. There was also a shot at baggage claim as they stood next to a row of motel telephones.

I hopped a few shuttles; the third one to a motel where the clerk looked at the photo and said "You are the third guy checking on them. Why are they so popular?" I didn't answer, but got a similar comment when I stopped by the Alaska Marine Highway ticket office. It was a good day's work, except for my wondering what the credit card bill would be. As we flew back to San Diego, I mentioned to my wife that maybe we should plan a cruise to Alaska as our next trip.

Do Drop In Sometime

The whole business of trying to achieve a total change of identity follows a very basic idea: Never be or do anything you were or did before. Except perhaps where gender is involved. The concept seems easy in many ways, more difficult in others. You can change the brands of the products that you buy from jeans to aftershave, learn to like different foods, gain or lose weight, go to contacts or switch to glasses, thousands of little things that might be a clue to the real you. For example, your mom, with extreme difficulty, managed to avoid chocolate in any form except in the privacy of our home. I took to wearing a wristwatch rather than carrying it in a pocket. However, even if one is able to cover all the minutiae of daily life, there are some things that are more difficult to deal with. Such as height.

As you know, I am exactly six inches taller than your mom. And no one would ever mistake her for anything other than a very attractive lady, though she and size nine never did speak the same language. So what you have is a couple, male and female, of a certain age range and with a specific difference in height. Those factors do eliminate a lot of other couples when a searcher starts looking at people in a community.

We tried to narrow the risk somewhat by being seen together in public very rarely. When we were, we tried to remember not to stand next to each other or to sit as quickly as possible when in a restaurant. To occupy our time we soon decided to spend a lot of time enjoying the outdoors all around our new home. Hiking rain or shine with more rain than shine on the many area trails seemed to be a good way to be together while also keeping in shape and it seemed to be one thing we could do without too much concern about being found. Or so we thought.

Then, sometime after we were here for about a year, that changed. When we made our almost daily hike, we tried to avoid trails like Perseverance and East Glacier where the most people seemed to go. And most of the tourists that got out of downtown seemed to gravitate to the Mendenhall Glacier Visitor Center area where the East Glacier trail starts. We also tried to hike when the trail traffic was lighter, such as on weekdays. And to stay away from places like Outer Point Trail when the tourist season was in full bloom, as there was always the chance that someone from the past might show up here in tourist country and take a guided hike. We also soon became aware that while you might see someone along the trail who you know or recognize, you seldom see the same person two days in a row even on the same trail at the same time. Joggers and dedicated dog walkers seemed to be the only exception to this.

The only earlier 'early warning' that we had about someone possibly looking for us was about three months after we arrived and were perhaps feeling more relaxed than we should have been. We were having breakfast at Donna's Restaurant out in the valley on Glacier Highway and were at a table away from the gaggle of guys having their coffee and maple bars at the counter. The same ones were there almost every day almost like they were, in navy lingo, plank holders. One of them was the driver of the blue bus that had taken us into town when we got here. As he got up to pay his check, he came over to our table, said hello, and asked how we were enjoying life in Juneau. We chatted for a few minutes about how much we were enjoying things here. Then he asked "Did your friends find you?"

Mom replied, "What friends?"

He told us that two different guys had ridden the bus since we arrived and talked to him about trying to meet up with us. As, each time, the questions seemed a bit too smooth, he hadn't said anything beyond, "Lots of people ride into town, can't recall a couple like that specifically, tourist season and all. Neither guy was willing to give me a card or phone number. Enough not said to not say much. And you folks looked a bit stressed, not like the usual visitors or folks I know arriving home."

We thanked him for the heads up and said it might have been former neighbors we hadn't written to yet. Or maybe Ed McMahon trying to bring us a check. As he ambled out, Mom took my hand under the table and gripped it tightly.

That's why our curiosity was raised several months later when we ran across two hikers, a male and a female, two days in a row when we were out on the West Glacier Trail one day and doing the Lemon Creek Trail the next day. They had daypacks on, had a dog along, and passed us on each trail as we took a break to see who might pass us. Nothing much was said other than hi, nice day, sure is, and on up the trail. Perhaps because the couple looked so normal, they were not. We had a long discussion after the second encounter about possible paranoia on our part.   There are over ninety trails in the 4,200 square mile borough, both trails we had been on were in the valley area and maybe four miles apart.   Also, we selected the trail of the day after leaving to hike with no word left with anyone. Most importantly, we went by bus and then walked up to several miles to arrive at the trailheads.

The incident at Donna's and seeing the same couple two days in a row were things we mentally logged in as being curious, but we didn't know how much we should be concerned about. We concluded that we should be concerned about everything, but not become too worried without more facts. Then we came home one evening planning to pick up the dog we were house-sitting for and head out on a hike. At the time we were on a one-month sitting stint at a house near Auke Bay, close to the start of the Spaulding Trail. It was a short walk one direction to the post office and not far the other way to DeHart's Store by the boat harbor. Just before the trailhead parking, Seaview Drive leads to several homes that back up to the first part of the trail. The location was ideal, as we could walk out the backdoor and be on the trail, which was the good thing. The not so good thing was that it allowed easy access to our backyard. As we drove into the yard that afternoon, we expected the black lab to be barking and ready to go. Instead, he was in a deep sleep and not trying to pull his chain off the run. When we could not wake him, I went in and called the vet, then loaded the eighty pounds of dog into the car, and headed back to town.

As we drove, the dog seemed to wake up slowly. By the time we made the Fred Meyer turn, off Egan

Drive onto Glacier Highway, and parked at the clinic, the dog was almost back to normal. The vet went ahead with a checkup and found nothing wrong. We felt chagrined about making it an emergency as the vet asked about food, water, and toilet tendencies. "Had anybody given the dog a sedative?" he asked.

"Why would anyone, he isn't a barker or a vicious dog, just Old Rex," I replied.

"Have you checked your house?" was his next question.

"No," I answered, "we wanted to get here."

"Just keep an eye on him and call me if anything else happens with him," the vet said.

We headed back home and checked around the house carefully, after cautiously entering it. There was nothing noticeable to make us think the place had been searched, just a feeling, and maybe some dust lines that did not match. If someone had been there, it had to be somebody that knew how to search without being obvious. We went out into the fading sunlight and walked around the yard, as the now fully awake dog romped around us. Out past where the firewood was stored we found faint boot tracks coming and going to the nearby trail. It was possible to hike the trail and take a detour into our yard and house. Happy hunting; there was nothing in the house to find. Yet it was like a call to general quarters back in my navy days. Apparently 'they' had found us or thought it was us and were checking further. So the frequent moves had been figured out. Not that it mattered; we were moving on to a new place in a week anyway. The fact that we had not yet been directly contacted or harmed seemed to indicate that we were in a stalemate - except that we had an edge, in that we knew where the film was and 'they' didn't. 'They' also could not know what kind of fallout might result if we were harmed.

Our choice was to try what Mom called 'Plan B' to see if the couple showed up again and if they knew the finer nuances of the trail system. The next afternoon, we rode a city bus to the downtown area and got off in front of the state capitol. From there we headed over to Gold Street and uphill, then over to Basin Road and on to the start of the Perseverance Trail. As we crossed a steel-grated bridge and stopped at the overlook at the top of the first uphill stretch, we didn't see anyone coming up behind us. We hiked on up past the place where Ebner Falls could be seen cascading down from just below where we were headed. This part of the trail runs as straight as any trail in the area and it seemed there was still no one behind us on the trail.

A few minutes later, we turned right off the trail and headed down a rocky path to the cleared area overlooking the falls. Without stopping, we forded the small stream to the right, edged our way along the steep bank overlooking the falls and headed for the old trail leading back to the main trail. As we passed mining era relics and approached the main trail, we stopped and listened. There was the sound of hikers hurrying up the trail we had been on just minutes earlier. As soon as they passed and were headed down the side trail to the falls area, we stepped out and headed back down the trail.

When we came to a place where we could see the parking area at the end of the road, I could see a plain Ford sedan sitting there. We took the other trail fork back toward the road and then bushwhacked our way uphill toward an older, mostly unbrushed trail used mainly by bird watchers. That led us to where we could follow the plank-covered Gold Creek water supply channel. We eventually came out between two houses in the older part of Juneau above the cemetery where the guy that the city is named after is buried. Our hunters were probably still wondering if we had gone over the falls or found a way to cross the log that spans the gorge near where the falls fall.

With this confirmation that someone was really keeping a close eye on us, we talked over whether the next part of Plan B was in order. Reluctantly, we decided to go ahead. The next evening, toward sundown, we headed for the trail that goes through what was the city of Treadwell in the abandoned mining area south of Douglas. When the city of Treadwell had a population of 5,000 many years ago, work in the mines went on around the clock every day of the year except July 4 and December 25. The era ended when a mineshaft drilled out under the channel flooded and collapsed in 1917. Since then it's been all history and ghosts. Now the people in Douglas mainly work across the bridge in Juneau, and Treadwell slumbers in ruins along the beach to the south. Our thought was to use a part of the area history and maybe some of the thirty-four ghosts in one part of the ruins to check out whether someone was on to us.

We took the last city bus of the day out to the end of the line in Douglas where it turns around at the end of St. Ann's Avenue. No one was in sight when we got off the bus. After it pulled out and headed back to town, we did not see any cars arriving in the area as we started down the trail. Lights were just coming on in some of the homes that are above the trail for the first few hundred feet. Minutes later we came to a place where the trail goes left toward the old mining buildings and the beach or right and uphill toward the Glory Hole. We glanced back and saw a couple hiking toward us in the gathering dusk. Even without the dog, it appeared to be the same two people who had passed us on the other trails. Back to height and gender. The idea was to hike up to the edge of the Glory Hole where the trail section ended and perhaps get a good look at the followers. Maybe we would even ask them directly if they were following us. Otherwise, we would try to follow the edge of the Glory Hole to where a faint path led down to the ruins of a concrete building we had explored while walking the lower trail.

Trying to appear casual, we headed on up the trail to the right. We stopped a few times to examine plants, mining relics, and to appear as if everything was normal. Then, when we were about one hundred feet from the Glory Hole, we suddenly started running for our lives. We heard the couple behind us also start running, which did not quite fit the image of normal hikers. I glanced back once and saw the man raise what appeared to be a pistol. My speed increased as Mom barely managed to keep up. The thought about the pistol was confirmed when three shots rang out and whizzed just over our heads. "They're shooting at us," Mom gasped.

"You noticed!" I replied. "Let's hide."

As we scrambled up the slope with our hearts pounding wildly, darkness descended on us. Our goal was the Glory Hole, where miners had once dug down to open-pit mine for gold. Thirty-four of them died on the job back when worker's compensation didn't exist. Later, the deep water-filled pit became a place to dispose of automobile remains. At last we got to the point where the trail ends abruptly with a drop of about three hundred feet into the icy water of the Glory Hole. Swerving left at the last second, we balanced on a narrow ledge for a few feet and entered the back of the small tree root caves where kids could crawl through to look down into the water. Our panting was loud enough that the couple chasing us probably would have no trouble finding us.

Our pursuers apparently were not aware of our change of direction in the dark or did not turn quickly enough. They continued straight ahead. By the time they realized we were not in front of them, that the trail ended quite abruptly, and perhaps tried to stop, it was too late. We heard the man utter a two-word six-letter descriptive phrase and the woman screamed. Then the night sounds around us briefly included more screams followed by thunks as the couple landed on the junk cars long relegated to the Glory Hole by Douglas folks, a splish -splash as they slid off into the water, then only silence.

As we crouched in the cave, I wondered why the fools didn't stop, why did he shoot, what was going on? Should we have planned better? Then Mom almost calmly reminded me that the shots might bring the police, which wouldn't help us stay unnoticed.

After waiting briefly to see if the noise had caused anyone to come to investigate, and also to see if the couple had someone backing them up, we emerged from the caves still very shaken but even more cautious. Taking a faint path to the right, we climbed down the concrete ruins there and soon crossed the main trail. We managed to find our way down through the dense undergrowth to Sandy Beach. After waiting in the shadows for a few minutes, we walked separately back toward Douglas through the Savikko Park rec area and then went one at a time up to Fifth Street and on to the Mt. Jumbo Trail. Getting up the first part of the trail in darkness without using a flashlight was a minor miracle that we somehow accomplished; it's a challenge even in daylight.

Our overnight accommodations were among the welcoming bugs near Parris Creek. Next morning, we hiked the Treadwell Ditch Trail and kept going until we came out of the woods on the Eagle Creek Trail out on North Douglas Highway. A city bus picked us up; the driver was a different one so at least we were lucky on that.

Several days passed before the bodies were noticed floating in the waters of the Glory Hole. The Search and Rescue folks had a difficult time descending down into the hole and recovering the bodies while perched on the hood of one of the derelict cars. The local paper later reported the hiking accident as a tragic event apparently involving two tourists not familiar with the area. Identification was never made, as the bodies did not have any identification, no fingerprint reports ever showed up, and no one made a missing persons report. The clothes and backpacks had no labels on them and the gun was apparently now at the bottom of the Glory Hole. The car they were apparently using was found parked a block from the trailhead where the bus we were on would have passed. It had been sold for cash a few months earlier and title had never been transferred, as the former owner headed 'outside.' It might not have been found except for a homeowner on St. Ann's Avenue who was worried about someone using his coveted parking spot.

As time passed, the case was filed away by the police and ultimately a fence was erected at the drop-off point. We had no way of knowing whether the couple had been a real threat. If so, had they reported to anyone? Of the three possible organizations that might have located us, only one probably traveled with no identification. That seemed to indicate that the hikers may have been from the group that would prefer us more dead than alive. Regrets? Absolutely - coupled with the us or them thoughts. We didn't ask to become involved in this situation anyway. Now we became even more cautious.

SUNSHINE - IN RETROSPECT

The rent-a-couple that hit the water in the Glory Hole caused an unexpected setback in my search. With their help, I was now sure that I was on the right track with the right people in my sights. My helpers had finally focused on a couple that fit the profile for age, size and gender and seemed to be out on one trail or another almost every day. The time that they hiked late on weekdays seemed to indicate that at least one of them was working at a day job someplace. But before making any move, I wanted to make absolutely sure.

The problem was that the couple had cover and identities that seemed foolproof. With my helper's assistance in doing some basic background investigation, some other things were learned. Such as that both identifications were valid, the social security numbers were solid, and even their driver's licenses and club memberships all checked out. But the fact was that who they were now was not who they were when they were tourists in San Diego. At least the names were different. How could they have arranged all of that on short notice? I knew that there were certainly ways to get new identity packages made up, but how would two ordinary people have done that almost overnight? Were they getting help from someone or some agency outside of here?

Along with that question was the need to know if they had the film and knew what was on it. If not, where was it? I did not want to do anything without knowing what other events might be triggered if and when I played my hand. That's why I had called for backup in the form of a couple to hike the local trails and do some of the other legwork so that I could stay in the background. I needed them to do the finding and then to see what the quarry's habits were and maybe pick up a pattern that would lead to a hiding place. Of course, I didn't meet them face-to-face when they arrived at the airport. They were not hard to spot when they came off the plane, as they did not fit the profile of the average tourists and no one was waiting to greet them. They probably didn't realize that the guy next to them at the baggage belt would call them after they were checked in at their motel. By the time they arrived I had rented the place on Glacier Avenue and set up light housekeeping. Though I had a phone there, my only contacts with them were by random telephone calls from pay phones. No one knowingly sees Sunshine face-to-face on an assignment, even when they don't know I am involved.

With their help, I finally solved the puzzle as to what the target couple was up to as far as living arrangements. Each time I or my helpers thought we had a fix on them, we didn't. When they drove somewhere, the car never seemed to be the same one more than once or twice. Watching a house where they were living would suddenly result in watching other people come and go and learning that they were the real homeowners. Then it was back to finding where the people who had been there were living now.

Then it finally dawned on us that maybe they were just staying in the various places while the owners were out of town. That would explain the moving in and out, car changes, and no record of any home ownership and maybe their post office habits. The four places where they could pick up mail didn't show a box being rented. Their trips to check for mail coming general delivery seemed to be geared to the month of the year so that no pattern of coming and going could be firmly set. Sort of like "If it's February it must be the Douglas post office," but not for sure. Maybe it was a way for some outside person to keep in touch with them, or it could have just been an effort to avoid junk mail.

The couple I had called in were two ex-cops who had bailed out of police careers after becoming bored with patrol car life and slow promotion rates. Where was the excitement of the TV cop shows? As private investigators, they hoped for more thrills in their work. Well, maybe they found it here at least once. Of course, before that they had to learn the basics of trailing and shadowing all over again. It's one thing to follow someone in an urban or city setting where there are lots of people and cars around that all look the same. There's a world of difference up here where there are less cars and people, but more wild animals to add to the blend. In one way it's easier, because if you have an idea which way the people headed by car, many of the possible trailheads can be checked quickly by driving a loop pattern. If they went by bus, it became more of an effort to pass the bus and wait near the next trailhead to see if they got off. A lot of the trailheads were right off the route. A few of the possible destinations, like the Nature Trail, might require a detour to check out.

The other consideration was whether someone concerned about being followed might duck off the trail into the underbrush and watch to see who else came up the trail. As a practical matter, that does not work too well. Before the helpers arrived, I had tried to make a few pit stops while on long hikes and learned some basic facts during the painful efforts. The rain forest has a lot of rotting fallen trees, low branches, and other snares. The debris is mixed with rampant vegetation, the most common being the acres of Devil's Club, which grows at all heights. If these things are overcome, there is always a wet or muddy place to sink into. When these natural obstacles are combined with occasional open mine shafts and diggings, it's better to stay close to the trail.

The helpers did a good job for the most part once they learned the basics, got lots of exercise and more than a few bites from white sox, no seeums, and other native insects. While the couple was good at following, they apparently got too close a few times. Juneau doesn't have too many loop trails, so most times you come back the same way you went. The pair learned one of the exceptions the hard way out in the Granite Creek Basin. They spent a long afternoon waiting to spot the other couple coming back down the trail to where it joins Perseverance Trail. What they didn't realize till later was that their subjects had decided to hike the ridge line and come down the Mt. Juneau and Perseverance trails back to Basin Road.

After that I suggested that they get more familiar with the local trail guides. Apparently they did not, or they would have known more about the Glory Hole. When the lesson was learned the hard way for them, I realized that the quarries' state of alertness did confirm my opinion as to who they were. The shots fired were way outside of the instructions I had given the couple. I didn't even know they were packing weapons. The whole scene was so stupid. Not to mention area residents calling the police about their sleep being disturbed so close to sundown. Of course this did not answer the change of identity questions or answer where the film was. Any other searchers now in town were probably wondering the same thing.

I continued to do my daily duties as I pondered my next move.

THE FIRST LADY

When my press person prepared an official biography of my life and times, first as a presidential candidate's wife and later as the incoming First Lady, it was a fairly straightforward task. Born in a mid-size town in the upper middle-west into an upper middle-income family, good grades in high school, but not the class valedictorian. Summer camps with horseback riding, canoes, and unofficial visits from the guys at the next camp. Everything was out in plain sight, nothing unusual, study hard, set goals, eventually plan to meet the future husband, live even beyond the American Dream of a family and financial security. On to a better than better college to prepare for law school. No serious romances along the way to marriage, but a few great crushes. Spend some time doing the funny glasses and unshaved legs feminist role for a while, but no public bra burning. That would not fit the proper future image. Meet a fellow law student along the way, marry him after graduation with the proper major production wedding, go through the bar exam ritual, embark on our law careers as he shows an interest in politics. Eventually he gets all the way to the highest office in the land, Mr. President, and I become First Lady. The rest, as they say, is history.

Except that a few chapters were left out of the official story because the author and almost everyone else have no idea that those chapters exist. And most likely never will.

In a legal sense, my putative parents, much as I loved them over the years, were simply parties to a contractual arrangement that gave them a secure financial future. In return for being provided a business that was set up for them, a home in the city they moved to soon after my birth, and all the extras, my 'parents' took on their roles as I left a very private hospital soon after a normal birth. My real mother went on her way back into her own 'family' where she could later enter into a properly arranged marriage with the son of another family unit. That would have been impossible if she had been encumbered with a child born out of wedlock. I've always thought it interesting that a family of families so involved in illegitimate ventures should not want to acknowledge a child that fit the same description. Anyway, from the time I was born, I was intended to be in what the spy novels call 'deep cover.'

I don't think there was any real plan for my future at the time the whole charade started. Aside from resolving an unplanned pregnancy, it was more like making an investment that might pay off in some unexpected way in the future. My only early awareness that something was not quite normal came when I was old enough to be told that I had a second set of grandparents, but that I was never, ever, to tell anyone about it. We did visit them at least once every year at a very secure lodge they owned in upstate New York. They were nice to me and my parents, but it's hard to know people when you can't call or write, and have only an occasional visit.

Then, as I completed college and my pre-law studies, a more definite plan began to emerge, a way that I could possibly provide a return on the investment in my raising and education without acknowledging my true family ties. Perhaps at some point I could emerge from my deep cover and provide a return on the investment.

There was in that era an annual nationwide high school speaking contest where the regional winners, all male and sponsored by a church organization, were awarded a trip to Washington and the opportunity to meet the president. It is perhaps a bit ironic that the one photographed shaking hands with the president, then best known for his lustful wanderings, should later become even better known for his doings in that same arena.

There must have been something in that picture that caught the eye of someone in my real family, perhaps a glint of ambition coupled with a willingness to push to the limits of what was right. Also, the young guy was not bad looking for a teenager. As a result of whatever the wire service picture revealed, I was launched on a long shot collision course that later got me accepted into the same law school class as that former teenager. At least along the way he had managed to avoid going to war and perhaps missing his destiny. I played my cards right, set the bait without being obvious, didn't get too far into the blatant feminist role, but showed that I was able to think for myself. The hook was set and, after a reasonable amount of resistance, the prize was on board. But who caught who? The best part of it was that he is the type of guy that I would have been attracted to anyway, nice looking, but not handsome in a Hollywood way, and a listener, thinker, and friend.

Perhaps he saw me as the type of strong, supportive woman that he needed to balance his personality and fit into his career plans, not Miss America, but nice enough and someone who would age well. Or as one that would perhaps understand his need to prove himself capable of attracting women without being tossed out on his ear each time that a new rumor surfaced. After all, that much tossing would have left him constantly bruised. Better to accept publicly, deal with him the way only a woman can, and plan for the future, his and mine.

However, a woman can only accept that type of life for so long and then it's so long or take some other action. Which is why I suggested the filming project as a way for my 'family' to get into a position of greater influence. Of course, no one knows better than me what type of woman he is attracted to. What I really wanted to do, though, was to slow him down just a bit, at least until we were through with the White House years. At the same time, if the pictures turned out well, then both my families, past and present, and I would benefit.

When he returned to the hotel room that night in San Diego, it seemed like the plan had worked. But like any good plan that involves humans, it takes only one weak link in the chain. If the photographer had just fulfilled his contractual obligations rather than try to unilaterally modify the contract, mutual satisfaction would have been achieved.

Bonk: Another Poker Game

I was still at a loss as to how to blindside Ernie with what I had learned on my trip to talk to the boys. Nobody back there seemed worried about the couple being gone. The kids talked in circles like the folks had maybe gone off to join the Peace Corps or went off on a church mission or maybe were building Habitat For Humanity houses in deepest Africa. I had my doubts about those theories and the casual attitude at the man's office about "We'll see him when he gets back." The only guys I know of who can leave their jobs for months or years at a time and continue to be paid are politicians running for president.

However, the picture showing the father and Ernie in a navy officer's uniform at the Naval Training Center showed some connection, past and maybe present, between the two. The fact that the Blazer Ernie owned went north to Seattle at a certain time seemed a likely indication of something other than a man, a woman, and health coverage even if the joke was funny. I arranged to get a copy of the photograph to trap Ernie with.

When the next poker night came around, I made sure that I was early so that I could hang the picture on the wall directly behind where I usually sit and across from his lucky chair. I didn't say anything about it when he walked in and joined the rest of us. At one point early in the game I did see him glance up toward the picture, then concentrate again on his cards. Somehow I sensed that it was a real test of his will power for him to not say anything and to continue to play his hands well. There was no comment till later when the other guys were out for a mid-game break and I was the one who gave in.

I finally spoke. "The term an attorney might use would be 'nexus.' A connection or link between events or facts. For some reason, a picture is there on the wall. It was not there last week. If it has any nexus or bearing on anything about anything, legal ethics and rules about privacy of attorney/client communications would enter into discussion of it. And, of course, an attorney could not comment on any representation without consent of the client."

I continued. "Someone saw a body and maybe the person or persons responsible for a murder. The same someone may have something, say a roll of film, that led to the killing. Or that might explain the killing. But the person with the film is not a witness to anything except what was at a murder scene. The film, in and of itself, does not show anything about how the person was killed. It may explain the why and show a motive, but to use motive, you need to find the killers and build a case against them. The film may be the first step in that process, but motive is already there: someone wanted some film or any prints made from it. As there is motive already; finding the film would only add to it. Whoever had the pictures taken may be remotely involved in a conspiracy of some sort. The intent of the picture taking was not to commit murder but may have led to it. It may have involved invasion of privacy or lead to some other acts which might be criminal in nature. Finding the film could lead backwards to other possibly criminal acts which were never carried out and produce links to someone directing the killers. That opens up a whole lot of other possibilities. How about intent to interfere with the due process of government? That's done all the time in many ways. Or as an effort to get leverage to make the Justice Department lighten up. But that happens in a lot of semi-legal ways."

He sat there listening to me ramble. Then he said, "When are you planning to take the bar exam? You seem to have a good grasp of some basic legal concepts. But let me tell you about the couple that kept going to the doctor's office...."

I felt like banging my head against the wall. It was like being subjected to a pitch by a salesman where, at a specific point, the next person to speak loses. When we left after the game, I took the picture with me. I've handled my share of interrogations of hard case criminals, but never before encountered anyone as hard to deal with as Ernie.

SUNSHINE - BINGO

After more than a year of searching without much to show for it except the fiasco at the Glory Hole, I needed to find some way beyond my present efforts as 'they' were not making my job very easy. The Glory Hole couple had made reports by telephone when I called them, but not in enough detail for me to pick up where they had 'dropped off'. My targets had not rented a place or done anything under their own names. I was sure that I had located them, but needed the last bit of proof before taking the next step. They resembled a lot of couples, tourist and otherwise, that fit the basic profile, though most of the tourists were somewhat older, less mobile, and left town in a matter of hours. It was really like looking for the right needle in a tree -filled haystack.

Finally after another round of explaining to my employer about ongoing per diem expenses and more commuting to see my wife and family, I began to daydream about a move that would allow the search to continue indefinitely while eliminating the per diem and commuting. I could go back to work in a second and more visible job as an officer on the local police force. There was a spot that had been left vacant by an early retirement for health reasons. None of the other officers were yet eligible for the job. Maybe I could feel more like I was where I belonged job-wise. If at some time I needed to act to complete my original task, I could deal with the conflict of interest issue at that time. So, what if, out of the blue, we, wife and I, pulled up stakes, left the relatives behind to gossip about us, and were on the way to sometime qualify for PFDs. We could even get our own roll of duct tape and a blue tarp to celebrate our new status as Alaskans.

What if....?

While I was thinking of how I could convince my wife that such a move was the right thing for us to do and that I was not suffering from cabin fever, I finally took another trip to the couple's stateside home for an even more detailed search. The clutter indicated that the two sons were still in college and not reading Good Housekeeping magazine. This search didn't take long and showed me that maybe my skills are not what they once were. I hit pay dirt in less than an hour in a spot where I was sure I had looked before. Or maybe it was more obvious now because I was looking in a different direction for some reason to explain why they were so determined to stay out of sight.

In a small brown molded box with Boy Scout emblems on it that I found buried at the back of a bureau drawer was a high school class ring that looked hardly worn. That simple almost hidden memento had the name of a high school and the year engraved on it. I placed it back in the box and the box back where it had been and left the house. Maybe this would be my last service call here. As soon as I was back at my motel, I connected my laptop to the connection in my room, logged on to the internet, and started researching alumni activities at high schools around the country. I already realized that the birthstone in the ring didn't match the one for the month on the husband's official birth certificate. My computer efforts led to only three high schools with the name on the ring. It was time to go look at yearbooks starting with the year he went into the service.

The next morning I checked out and headed for the airport. After more flying time, the second school I visited was where I struck it rich. There, though a much younger version with more hair, much thinner and with a different name, he was. A middle of the class graduate with no great honors recorded and expected to become famous as a writer or actor. My call to the one phone number in the local directory with his family name was answered by an uncle. I said that I was an old classmate of his nephew trying to locate old friends. The uncle said bluntly, "He left town after the memorial service for his parents. None of us ever heard from him after that. Never a word. We have pretty much given up. We all understood what he was going through, but he would not talk about it. If you find him, tell him to call."

I visited the local newspaper and found the rest of the answer in the microfilmed archives. The story of gangland violence on a long ago summer evening far from home was a mirror of similar events that had motivated my present career. It had even taken place when I was a rookie not too far from the city where it had happened. I had about that time witnessed a similar scene. Both carnage scenes were the type of thing that leaves a forever imprint on the soul, the stuff of 3 a.m. wide awake thoughts. So, as a result of his, he had just dropped out. But where to and with what help? Where would a full background cover package with new identification come from? There was only one federal outfit that I could think of that ever did things like that.

Somehow he surfaced in San Diego at the Naval Training Center with a different name, later went on to college and then married. If what I was thinking was what did happen, then what could I tell the people I work for? This is really, like Yogi said, déjà vu all over again. I flew home, reminded my wife of the bible verse about 'whither thou goes' and then headed back to the search.

I had a lot of time to think while cooped up in the big bird winging its way toward Seattle and then taking the Alaska Airlines flight on to Juneau. After figuring out that the guy was not now who he was when he got to San Diego on vacation and was not then who he was when he was in high school, the wheels started to fall into place like three cherries on a slot machine. I could understand the latest change, what with bodies being found here and there and with various people on his tail. The swiftness of how he managed to disappear still puzzled me though. If he was by some chance under a witness protection program, the feds don't work that quickly or efficiently, though the end result might have been more professional. And such a move probably would have included the kids. The earlier change before he started a family had more of the imprint of federal involvement; a sudden total disappearance after testifying, no contact with surviving relatives, a new life with no trace of the earlier one - except for the class ring that I had found.

What I thought about most between takeoffs, beverage services, mini-meals, and 'prepare the cabin for landing' announcements was how much his journey was like mine. We had both encountered extremes of violence and found our futures formed as a result of it. His encounter had finally led to happiness, even factoring in San Diego; mine had led me to work that found a way around the use of violence. Yet, if I was to continue this assignment, even the use of non-violent means could result in the death of two people who had not really done anything to earn such an end. If I went ahead, was I just being an agent of the callousness that I was so opposed to?

Maybe the Big Guy up there somewhere would forgive me for what I had done so far in my life, but not for doing that. Or was this what is known as a mid-life crisis? Yet if I didn't do it, someone else might do what I couldn't - and not as neatly. But the thought of those kids who had probably taken their parents to the airport and now waited for a someday safe return surely deserved more than they would get if I continued my assignment.

On a different level, this had turned out to not be the type of assignment I had thought it would be. My working arrangement was that, except for expenses, I didn't get paid for dispatching unless it was completed with no adverse publicity. There were also cancellation provisions in the event conditions changed so that I could be compensated for time spent on the matter.

In this situation, the basic budget for the original operation was based on a cost/benefit ratio as now adjusted for the extra expense incurred when the photographer tried to renegotiate, assignment of staff to resolve that, the photo shop debacle, and my contract price, had caught the attention of the bean counters. They were apparently crunching numbers and telling management that the point had been reached where the fiscal picture showed it was time to cut losses and move on to other projects with greater potential. You are not in business to lose money. If this project later shows an actual return without further investment, so be it.

Then, like one of those epiphany things the priests used to like to talk about, or maybe it was the plane landing in Seattle before I caught the Juneau flight, my decision was made. All I had to do now was convince my wife to move from where she had lived all of her life. No big deal, she would like the change. The selling points would be my having a job that didn't involve a lot of travel, being far away from some members of the family except for summer visits, and better weather and less traffic. That's how I came to be a line officer, training and patrol supervision, in Juneau, and made a lot of new friends. The wife is happy quilting up a storm, learning a lot of ways to fix halibut and salmon, and has even talked me into attending church at St. Paul's on Sunday. But I am not sure that I want to take confession yet; time needed and not wanting to overwhelm the priest figures into that.

I was able to end my efforts without any difficulty or ill will. The company even sent a nice monetary gift to acknowledge my second retirement. Now I moved into the role of guardian angel over the people I had been sent to find and possibly dispatch. Someone else might be out there still hunting. I knew that they had an unlimited budget, a per diem allowance, and were still charged with protection of the subject of the photography. Whether protection stopped at prevention of physical harm or extended to perceived threats to public opinion was a question I couldn't answer. The couple would not know that my efforts had ended and that the greater danger was from the guys in the white hats. They needed someone to watch their backsides. Me.

BONK - CRUISING ALONG

The trip we took to Seattle made my wife aware that if we traveled I was likely to want to spend time schmoozing in the local cop shops, which would allow her to have lots of time to pursue her hobby of shopping. Maybe I have spent too many years on the job; I tend to people watch and wonder how an area would be patrolled rather than shop for stuff I could buy for less back home and don't need anyway. When I suggested the basic seven-day Alaska cruise to Juneau and back, her first questions were about the shops there and on the cruise ship.

We used some of our airline miles for the flight up to Seattle, overnighted there, and boarded the ship to head north. The ship was like a floating city with restaurants, lounges, non-stop entertainment, and games like bingo for the less lively travelers. The wife did manage to make a small dent in the inventory of the on-board shops and at the places we stopped along the way. I tried to relax and not worry about how much this party was costing that I couldn't claim as investigation expense.

When the cruise ship got to Juneau, we only had twelve hours in town and the wife wanted to do the tourist things. That meant that I had to watch and scope out the local scene as we toured. The only time that I could really poke around was a quick trip to the local cop shop in downtown for a short visit. I did manage to talk to a patrol sergeant on the day shift and he seemed very cordial, though my questions were unofficial. We talked for a while on his coffee break and I found that we were both career cops, though he had retired before getting back into it up in Alaska. He didn't think he could offer much help, what with the tourist season and lots of people in town. He did want a copy of the picture of the couple 'just in case.'

He promised that he would call me if he saw them around town. But why did I, with my cop nose shut down pretty much for vacation, seem to have a feeling that he had more interest than he was letting on. Oh well, on to the Red Dog Saloon for souvenirs and to meet the wife. You can't do Juneau without a visit to the Red Dog. Then we still had to finish her tour of the downtown shops and do the Salmon Bake tour before getting back to the ship.

Then, wonder of wonders, like old home week, though he didn't see us, as we were walking up Franklin Street looking into an store called The Foggy Mountain Shop, who did I see buying more warm gear but the assigned-to-Alaska Secret Service guy from San Diego. With him still here, maybe there was more fire than smoke. If the vibes from the police station were right, the couple was probably here outside of my jurisdiction. There was no hope of finding them in what was left of a twelve-hour port call.

PEEK-A-BOO BONK

When I got my marching orders to come up here, I didn't think that I would be able to last three weeks, let alone almost three years in Alaska of all places. I didn't ski, hunt, fish or hike till I got here. I sure do hike now, though. I may even have spotted the couple or one like them a few times at Fred Meyer and other places. A lot of couples seem to look like them. With the local dress code of rain gear and boots, who can tell? I would have trouble recognizing my own mother if she was dressed like the locals. Then, wonder of wonders, one afternoon while shopping for another new pair of hiking boots, what do these wandering eyes see outside the window of The Foggy Mountain Shop but the lieutenant from the San Diego Police Department looking in? The lady next to him with bags of stuff must be his wife. Are they here as tourists, or is something happening that I should be concerned about?

Since the last time I was in his town, I have become quite an expert photographer of the mining ruins and relics around here. The things I photograph are from the real hey day of mining in the Juneau area, which started somewhere around 1880. A few years later, Joe Juneau and Richard Harris were given grubstakes by George Pilz to look for gold around what became the Juneau area. Some stories say that the two traded much of the grubstake supplies for booze and native women, and that an Indian chief named Kowee almost had to point to where they could find gold. Over the next forty years, the race to extract gold from the streams and hills around the area was about the biggest thing happening here. In fact the town was even named Harris for a while.

The really booming part of the history in the Treadwell area, south of what is now Douglas across the channel from Juneau, ended in 1917 when a cave-in of a tunnel drilled under the channel brought the mining over on the island to a halt. Mining on the mainland continued to some extent until World War II finally ended it. There have been more recent mining activities out on Admiralty Island and a few other locations, but nothing like the boom days. Gold is found easier in tourist pockets these days.

My interest, as cover for my search, was in the ruins around Juneau and out on Douglas Island. When the weather permitted, I spent my days lugging my cameras around from place to place, day after day. There are usually trails to the places I was looking for, but getting off them to rummage for ruins led to a lot of interesting bouts with Devil's Club, mud, fallen trees, and collapsed mine buildings. After a while I began to enjoy the challenge. At times I even talk to hikers, which is sort of what I was sent here to do.

When the weather limited my range, I read, researched and actually started to come up with a really nice pictorial history of the area. The State Library in the State Office Building and the City Library down on the waterfront provided me with a lot of reading material, as did the owner of the antique book store called The Observatory up on

Second Street. One of the ladies that went along on a lot of the Saturday hikes with her husband worked at the city library and was a lot of help with my research. I was even starting to become known in the area as someone quite knowledgeable in the field.

I did try to locate the couple by using the 'looking for friends who got here first' routine on the driver of the bus that hauls people in from the ferry terminal out at Auke Bay. He either didn't know anything, or maybe did and wouldn't say anything without knowing why I was really asking. After that, I just kept hoping I would see the couple somewhere.

When I wasn't hiking on my own, I went along with the Parks and Recreation Saturday hikers.

Still, I still did not seem to be any closer to finding what I been sent here to find. There are just too many ordinary friendly people around here with none of them seeming to be on the run. Yet that's how I finally got my first break in the long search. The group had hiked up the Salmon Creek Trail to a spot above the dam that overlooks the huge pipe that carries water down toward the power generating station. As we ate our lunches and relaxed before starting the hike back, the talk shifted to a popular topic discussed quite often in this state. How much do you think the PFD check will be this fall? The oil revenue permanent fund annual dividend sent to residents living here a year or more is waited for with great anticipation each fall, and the amount it might be leads to a lot of speculation. It's like having a winning lottery ticket without knowing the date and amount. Whether you multiply $1,000 or $1,800 by one person or two people and six kids, it's a nice end of year treat to have.

As it was not a subject I could contribute much to, though by this time I had been here long enough to be eligible, I just sat and listened. Only two other people were silent during the conversation. My analytical mind picked up on this and I started wondering why the couple was silent. Usually they join right in talking up a storm with the rest of the group. I started to wonder why. Could this couple who seemed to have been here forever not be eligible for the dividend or have some reason for not applying for it? Maybe they needed a closer look.

I was also concerned, because for the last year or so the local radio station had started to play 'Everywhere you go, sunshine follows you' almost every sunny day, which at times isn't too often. The trade talk in the intelligence business is that the shadowy figure known as Sunshine is more than just another urban legend. The speculation is that his 'theme song' is often heard on the radio before he comes out of the shadows to do his work. With one station listened to by most of the residents, it would be much easier to get a request played than in a larger area. What a great way to announce the occasional day of sunshine and perhaps let his presence in the area be known.

Then there was the matter of the two people pulled out of the Glory Hole. I knew the area from my photographing the ruins around the Treadwell mining area and wondered if the couple found floating in the frigid waters of the Glory Hole had perhaps gotten too close to someone they were trailing. Who would the couple have been working for? Why were there no heirs charging forth to sue for wrongful death?

Of course, with the same type of luck that got me sent up here in the first place, my efforts to follow up on my lead led me to another unfortunate incident in my career. I figured that if I hiked the same trail my hiking group friends were on some evening, I might be able to talk to them as we hiked and see if my instincts were right. They had apparently headed up the Mt. Jumbo Trail late one afternoon, as I saw a car they used parked near the trailhead on Fifth Street in Douglas. My idea was to catch up with them and hike along as, after all, I knew them from the Parks and Rec group. I was hurrying along over the mud, rocks, and tree roots along the trail trying to catch up with them when they must have realized that someone was behind them. Maybe I should have called to them to let them know who it was. Or maybe they were skittish enough since the Glory Hole incident to be cautious of anyone coming up behind them. Anyway, the sun was starting to set and prudence should have told me to hike back rather than keep going. I ignored prudence and headed down toward the bridge over Parris Creek. In my hurry I remembered that some boards were missing but forgot which ones. I tripped, tried to regain my footing, and stepped through an opening. Somehow I ended up sitting on the bridge with one leg out ahead of me and the other through the opening in the bridge deck wedged firmly between the planks. It was probably better than having both feet go through or falling into the stream twenty feet below.

After I finally managed to extricate myself, I found that my scrapes and bruises were accompanied by a badly sprained ankle. I compounded my woes by next violating the FCC ban on using a marine radio when not on the water. Well, I was on a bridge over some water. I carried the radio in my daypack and figured under the circumstances I might be excused. I went to Channel 26, got the marine operator, and then the local police station. They were kind enough to send out a couple of volunteers from the local search and rescue group to help me get back to my car. One of them was a policeman that sometimes goes with us on the Saturday hikes. He made some comments about people who try to photograph scenery in the dark. Of course, my call for help was probably heard from Ketchikan to Skagway by every boater tuned to the channel, but at the time I didn't care. I just wanted to not spend the night out there. The couple must have kept going because they didn't come back while I was sitting out there. I decided that this was not a good way to scope them out anyway; it would be better to do that on the Saturday hikes after I recovered.

AMONG MY SOUVENIRS

My work as a member of the Washington D.C.
police force keeps me close to the White House,
though I don't normally socialize with the folks who
live there. I don't think that my late father did
either, though his work certainly showed up from
time to time in the daily intelligence briefings given
to the president. My dad was one of the unknown
real cold war warriors, having spent his career
traveling to the hot spots of particular recorded
moments in history after the event.   What he
accomplished along the way never made the evening
news,   though   it   certainly   would   have   been
newsworthy if made public.   His specialty, while
operating under a cover role as a travel writer, was
the detection and study of cold war assassination
weapons. If a world leader, dissident, or intelligence
agent died, he would be called. His job was to try to
determine the cause of death, how it was done, if not
by natural or obvious cause, and what method was
used. He would study the specifics of the weapon or
agent used and whether it might be something our
country might need in our arsenal. What he learned
was also helpful in better protecting our leaders.

After   the   cold   war   thawed,   his   workload
lightened   as   he   approached   and   went   into
retirement. When he died, my mother asked that I
go through his home office/nest where he would
retreat to reflect on the glory years he had enjoyed
but could not talk about. My own career was more

open if less dramatic. I had hopes of becoming an operative for the CIA or perhaps a Secret Service agent. However, even with a degree in police science and criminal justice, size and my gender kept doors from opening. At 5'4" and very female, I did not fit the mold. I was able, however, as the workplace became more enlightened, to succeed in police administration here in my hometown, which is a place where our president lives and moves around. That led to a lot of coordination of his protection with our local force, with me having the job of point person.

In that role, I not only worked with the Secret Service detail in planning times and routes, but was also aware of when various factors caused a higher level of watchfulness. My work was how I caught the roving eye of the current president, though he never did more than in a very discreet way acknowledge that in other times or places, we might have sung a duet from the same page of the songbook.

As he approached the end of his second term, I was invited to the White House where he and the First Lady were thanking people who had played minor roles in the smoother parts of his presidency. She must have somehow known of my dad's career, because as we chatted, she showed an interest in what my dad had done. I remember mentioning that I was still sorting through the stuff that Dad had accumulated, and that maybe some of it should go to the Smithsonian or some other place where people could see relics of the mid to late years of the past century, though some things perhaps had history best left unknown.

Perhaps I should have acted sooner, as shortly after the chat mother's house was broken into and a lot of the souvenirs disappeared. One of them was a very early version of the umbrella sting assassination weapon intended for use in public places as a way to kill without leaving a trace. The use involved a casual bump, an excuse me, and walking on. The victim would later become ill and die an agonizing death while doctors tried to figure out what had happened. Dad had shown it to me shortly before he died and told me of its history. I hoped that it had not been stolen by someone intending to use it. Mother did report the break-in to the police. She did not make an insurance claim, as it would be hard to figure replacement cost on the items. It would also be difficult to explain how the items were obtained.

THE FIRST LADY -

LOOKING TOWARD THE FUTURE

We were heading into the final year of our sojourn in Washington, at least in its present incarnation. The time was approaching when the media starts to list possible major accomplishments and setbacks of the administration. How can anyone on the outside ever have the audacity to speculate on what historians will be debating about far into the future? The skirmishes for who might be the next tenant of our house were in full swing, as they always are for two years prior to the next election. We had weathered the storms and were considering what next. In a sense, miles to go before darkness falls.

Apparently the plan I had suggested to gain leverage and to rein in Rambler had slowed him down and even made him more reflective. His roving eye still roved at times, but not with the impression that he was likely to follow up on the opportunities that were out there. He was more like an aging dog that eyes a passing car but does not chase it, only wondering what might have happened if he had caught it. As far as the leverage that had been hoped for, nada. The Secret Service contacts that I had didn't know that I knew about the film project. I did know that the agent who had been assigned to the family at the time had left on short notice for somewhere in Alaska and was still there. In any event, it was a bit late for leverage to be of any value.

There was a more serious consideration, however, that I was concerned about. Now that Rambler's tour in the spotlight was shifting to a lesser role, it was time for me to consider my future. A lot of the positive things that happened during our time here were things that we had talked together about long before they became promoted as administration policy. In effect, while he was the lead dog, it was really a team effort. Why not continue that team effort with me in the lead harness? Unless you are the lead dog, the view is always the same. I certainly have enough name recognition and ability to get elected to public office rather than practice law again and have to endure a flood of rancid attorney jokes.

The only fly in the ointment, so to speak, would be those photographs still out there somewhere. I could only imagine the jokes that would pop up if the pictures showed up while I was running for or was in office. Starting with "Do you know where your husband is tonight?" or, "I have to hand it to your husband." or worse. So now there was a real reason for them not to show up - aside from not being the best material for his presidential library.

About this time we were doing the social side of the long slide toward being on the way out while still being less than total lame ducks. It's the tea and cookie type thing with the fringe people who had helped make our time here go smoothly or might help me in the future. At one of the receptions, I was chatting with the lady from the D.C. police who interfaced with the Secret Service detail on our travels around town. In earlier times, she would have certainly been a prime candidate for extra attention by my helpmate.   After all, she is cute, blond, and female.   Not that any of that matters except the female part.

I knew that her late father had been a real cold war warrior.   Now she was wondering whether his souvenirs would ever have any value to a collector. Which is when my mind picked up on what she was talking about.   He had gathered and analyzed weapons of that era - and not just weapons, but things used to kill at close quarters without a trace. I told her that I had heard of a museum that collected such things and then moved on to chat with the other guests.

At the same time I was remembering who the agent in charge of the security detail had been on that long ago night in California.   Knowing what was about to happen that night, I had made sure that none of the family left our suite.   I had heard the elevator door open and people walking down the hall.   Did I imagine a whiff of perfume?   Shortly after that, there was more activity in the hall and the elevator doors opened again.   The timing seemed about right.   That was the night that Rambler came back late in such a somber mood, which carried over into the return trip from San Diego the next day.

The agent in charge didn't give me any details about anything happening except to allude to a security breach that had not resulted in any danger to the President.   Those guys really live up to "Don't Ask-Don't Tell."   I could tell him a few things that he would have trouble not telling.

Now, after considering various options, I decided to call the agent and see how he was enjoying his retirement.   I was also banking on his perhaps wanting to make up for allowing the 'security breach' on his watch, though my real reason was that the pictures were still out there somewhere. If he was not up to the task, perhaps he would know some other retiree who still yearned for the challenges of days gone by.

Before I could take any steps to further my plan, I needed to check on the status of the project that had at least led to some domestic tranquility in the White House over the past few years. As calls from our place are pretty much a matter of record, I waited until I made a trip to speak to a woman's group away from Washington.

After the luncheon and prior to making the speech, I excused myself from the head table to go to the lady's lounge. The place was posh enough to include a telephone in the anteroom. My escorting agent waited outside after checking to be sure the room was empty. I was able to make a quick call to the number I had memorized, punched in the extension number for the duty person, and quickly checked on the project status. The recorded message that came on advised me that the project was now inactive based on fiscal constraints and low potential value.   If I wished to speak to a customer service representative.... I hung up and left the room.

When I returned to Washington, I had my appointments secretary contact the agent who had headed the detail in San Diego. I said that I wanted to discuss details about the convention in case I ever wrote a book about these years. He agreed to stop by when he would be in town early the following week. When he arrived in my office, we chatted for a while about the time he had been in charge of the detail. He sipped coffee and answered my questions, which were all of a routine nature as my assistant took notes. After a while, I asked the assistant to go and check on some appointments that were scheduled for later in the day. After she left, I told the agent that there had been ongoing rumors about something that had happened that night.   He seemed hesitant to say anything.

I told him that I understood his position and that he might not want to give any details about that night because of the 'what goes on here stays here' and 'don't ask-don't tell' policies. So I said quite directly "If something did happen that night that you can't or won't discuss, I don't have any problem with that. However, I will say this. You were in charge of that detail. If there is any unfinished business, you have a duty, retired or not, to finish it. If something was taken, find it. That's all I will say. By the way, how's that guy doing that you arranged Alaska duty for? Is he still there? Has he caught any fish? Oh, and also, we were having a small reception here the other day. I was talking with that lady officer from the D.C. police force. Did you know about what her father did during the Cold War? Well it seems..." He left shortly after that after assuring me that I had nothing to be concerned about. No promises made or orders given, but maybe payback time will come when I am further along in my career.

The Encounter - Moving On

After the years of care and caution, what happened was the most simple way to be put back on the run. Mom had a toothache and went to see the dentist on Fourth Street near downtown. She had to be sedated and was not supposed to drive. A cab from the taxi place three blocks away should have been called. But I was just done with getting a haircut and called to see if she was ready to leave. I pulled into the Holy Trinity Church parking lot just across the street and waited for her to come out. As she came down the steps and crossed the street, I got out to open the door for her.

That's when a tourist couple stopped to unfold a city map, looked up, and called us by our own old names. It's good that it was not lunchtime when crowds of state workers might have been in the area to witness the scene. The couple with the map were from our home town, neighbors and PTA acquaintances now enjoying their cruise of a lifetime. They were looking for the gold-domed Russian Orthodox Church further up the hill and instead, they found us.

We, of course, couldn't deny who we were. I made some inane comment about having had a sudden job transfer, and we excused ourselves saying that I had to get Mom home so that she could lie down. We knew that, like most tourists, their time in town was short, so I said that we would call them at the end of their trip. They wanted to take a picture of us, but we quickly got in the car and drove away. I couldn't tell if they did take a picture as we drove away. We knew at that time that very likely we would have to move on, as the old domino effect was probably now in motion. "Guess who we ran into on our cruise, you would never believe it. We remember when they left on vacation and never came back, they gave us some wild story about a sudden job transfer, but that's hard to swallow. Wonder what really happened." If they called home while still on their cruise, our time to disappear might be even more limited.

Then, who might still be checking the house that we left behind? (Mom still misses her garden.) We were back in range and our exits were blocked. Air travel north or south became a matter of record airport to airport and the marine highway system is also easy to watch for people coming and going. This also happens to be the only state capital that no one can drive to or from. Not owning a boat and not wanting to try to hike over the ice into Canada made us realize that suddenly our security was also a trap. The house search and the Glory Hole incident came instantly back to our minds.

By the next day, we had decided to drop out and move on somehow rather than risk staying here any longer. After our over two years of apparent safety, the thought of running and always looking back was hard for both of us to accept. That's when we decided to 'go to ground' and hide where we knew the territory. The huts high up on the ridge south of town seemed like a good place to fall back to while we made further plans. Obviously, as winter approached, some other refuge would be needed.

The Forest Service public cabins offered some potential but had drawbacks. Access during the winter months would have to be by skis or snowshoes. And, while day use was allowed, people with reservations could bump us out at nightfall or on weekends. Constant use also might be a flag for any aerial searchers to send up a ground search party. For now, the shelters seemed the best choice.

Early the next morning, we loaded our backpacks, took them to the trailhead we planned to leave from, and hid them in the underbrush. We drove home, put the car in the garage, walked to the mall, and caught a bus to town. We hiked to the trailhead and were on our way to what we hoped was a safe haven. The trail up to the shelters was still as difficult as when we had first fought our way up to them shortly after we came here. Even though both of us were in much better shape now, our heavy backpacks and the steep terrain made the trek seem to last forever. There was no indication that anyone else had been on the trail since our last trip up this route.

The Saturday Parks and Rec hikers had been over the Sheep Creek part of the trail on one hike we did with them, but turned back shortly after starting up the slopes on the far side of the valley. This part of the trail then and now is so overgrown that it is impossible to see where it has eroded away and dropped off. On that hike, one just past middle-aged tourist had slipped and fallen, ending up head down in Devil's Club twenty feet below the trail. His distraught wife had tried to climb down after him, but calmer heads held her back as he was retrieved and checked out. There were no injuries except for a few scrapes on his backside and a few pieces of

Devil's Club that needed removing, but the hike leader decided not to hike any further.

We proceeded slowly, as our backpacks were loaded with food and water for staying at least a week. We would hike down to restock, and return or move on to a new home somewhere away from here. Our plans for the future were in limbo. We had finished a house-sitting stint just as we were leaving and had another one that could start in a week or so depending on whether the homeowners needed to fly out for medical treatment. I had arranged for leave at work and didn't know whether I would be going back. Mom had managed to get her library work covered as she had the same thought.

Our arrival at the second shelter was late in the afternoon. The sun was still high and a light breeze was keeping the smaller flying critters at bay. With mutual sighs of relief, we took off our heavy packs and started to set up primitive housekeeping. The Last Resort had not changed much, maybe a little more weather-beaten from the past few winters. Our choice was to sleep inside to thwart the local bear population, knowing that even inside voles and other small critters would be checking our food supply. Cooking was to be over a backpack stove, as we did not want to have a heating and cooking fire that might smoke and draw attention to our occupancy. Except for the shelter use, it was to be a real spike camp. Zipping our sleeping bags together would lessen the need for heat at night, though later in the season that would not be enough. A glorious sunset ended the first day of our new journey.

We passed the time by walking, reading, walking, journaling, and walking. We could see

Taku Inlet in the distance and occasional boats or cruise ships coming and going. This solitude lasted about two days, or maybe to the end of the first full day there. During the day we had retreated inside during the occasional times when a helicopter or light plane flew over along the ridge.

Sometime as the day was ending and we were preparing freeze-dried entrees on the small stove while trying to avoid insects commuting between us, Mom looked at me and said, "Enough of this. Camping is all right, but it doesn't solve the basic problem. I think we need to agree not to run any further, not retire to a place like this. Little House on the Prairie this is not. Not even the Walton's home place. Why not take our chances and see what happens? We've lasted for almost three years and we're set in a town with a good life here, even if it's not one hundred per cent of what we planned for. There have been people on our trail but no one, so far, has made a move to harm us. Maybe that's because any move against us might result in more damage to the other side. Even the man that shot at us near the Glory Hole probably wouldn't have if we had not been running away. The guy that was apparently caught on camera is now a very lame duck and any new revelations could barely top what has already been rumored."

Her common sense and determination seem to be what we needed to consider in deciding on the direction we headed. Tomorrow we hike back down, find out if the next house sitting is on or off, and go on with our lives, whatever happens next. We have decided how to end the matter of the film while staying safe. I am planning to hide this journal where it may be found someday in case we don't get back to retrieve it or to add a prologue to it. At least you will know what we planned to do.

As we packed the next morning to hike back to town, our spirits seemed lighter than they had been since the encounter. I told Mom about remembering something that I had read years back in "The Man In The Gray Flannel Suit" by Sloan Wilson. The man in the story told of his time in the service during World War II. His role was to go behind enemy lines in Italy by parachuting at night at low altitude over wooded mountain areas during the winter. It was not a good scenario for making future plans. To calm himself and prepare for the jump, he would say what might now be called a mantra. The three phrases to get himself out of the plane were, "It doesn't really matter." "Here goes nothing." and "It will be interesting to see what happens." Those words seemed to reflect where we were headed.

THE PLAN

Before we made the last journal entries, hid it, and left the shelter, our plans were discussed and re-discussed over several hours. We poked and prodded at them until things seemed as foolproof as two people could make them. The first step after I get back to work will be to visit the tourism people up on Level Eleven of the SOB to fill out a card so that the Alaska package will go to a potential tourist in San Diego. This was to alert Ernie to set up a conference call with us as our contingency plans allowed for.

Our basic plan is to proceed on an assumption that the Secret Service is the agency that would have the most interest in recovering the film. There was also an assumption that someone outside of the government had originated the plan to photograph whatever was on the film. Three unsolved murders in San Diego seemed to confirm that the filming wasn't just some local effort by the far right political action groups. We also know from some historical perspectives back as far as the Bay of Pigs aftermath that there may be times when the government, rightly or wrongly, may seek assistance from the less legal business organizations on the national scene. Of course the San Diego police might also be interested in learning why they had three unsolved murders on their books.

We have done our best to avoid encounters with the local police and have had only one since getting here. That one incident happened on a 'dark and stormy night' on a snow-slick Glacier Highway in Lemon Creek when a rear wheel departed from an ancient Datsun wagon we had been house-sitting for. I was struggling to find a spot to use a jack at some point where rust had not totally consumed the unibody metal. True Juneauites have an affinity for keeping such vehicles long past the expiration date, perhaps even after, if animals, they would be put to sleep. Mom was waving a flashlight while looking for the lug nuts that were somewhere in the snow near where we had slid to a stop minus the wheel and tire. The waving light also would warn any passing cars of our plight as they mushed through the snow. The first one headed our direction was a Juneau police car with two officers in it. They pulled behind our wounded wagon, activated the gum ball machine lights on top and offered to help us solve our problem. One of them had been along on several of our Saturday hikes on his day off and knew us from those times.

When Mom said that some lug bolts seemed to be AWOL, he told us not to worry. He said, "Remember the man who lost a wheel outside the fence of a mental institution? He was also looking for a way to bolt a wheel back on. A guy on the other side of the fence came over and suggested that he use one bolt from each of the other wheels as a way to reattach the wheel that had fallen off. The solution was simple and worked. When the man thanked the guy on the other side of the fence and asked why, if he was smart enough to figure the solution, was he behind the fence? The guy said 'I am in here because of a mental illness, not because of not being intelligent.' " The officers helped take a lug from each of the other three wheels, used a piece of wood from the trunk to help lift our wagon, and we were on our way - after checking the other wheels for tightness.

As that officer seems to be a local policeman with common sense, we have decided to see if he could help us solve our particular problem.

Sunshine - Through The Looking Glass

After nearly three years of looking for them, being sure that they were the ones I had been seeking, moving here to keep an eye on them, and finally being pulled off the assignment, as it had been dropped from the pending list for being of no present value, it was right back in my lap. I was no longer following my post-retirement career and was now quite happy being a Juneau police officer in the middle ranks. Juneau has far more accidental deaths than murders. The number of unsolved murders over ten years is probably less than what happened in San Diego in this case in just a few days. Aside from the usual death rate for a small community, we do lose quite a few cruise ship passengers each year, mostly from heart related things, as they enjoy their vacation of a lifetime.

The couple showed up at the station downtown one bright summer day. They said they had a problem that perhaps I could help solve. I had a fair idea of what they were about to tell me. It seemed that they had found something in San Diego three years earlier that might have involved them in a lot of trouble. Now they wanted to somehow contact various parties and wrap the matter up so they could go on with their lives. Their belief was that someone outside of the government had set up a plan to photograph whatever and whoever with whatever was on a roll of film that they had found.

Three unsolved murders in San Diego seemed to back that idea up. The San Diego police might be interested in knowing about who was responsible. If the Secret Service was the governmental agency interested in finding the film, perhaps they would have a way to contact and call off the people who wanted the pictures taken. How could they find a bridge to the different groups?

I told them that I was aware of a Secret Service agent who had been in the area for several years without seeming to have much to do except hike. He had called us on a marine radio about a year back from Parris Creek where he was stranded with a sprained ankle and other injuries. He had been hiking at sundown trying to observe two subjects of an ongoing investigation. He would not give any details about that. When he crossed the bridge trying to keep them in sight, he caught his foot as he fell through some missing boards and injured his ankle. The people he was watching apparently knew which boards were missing and avoided them in the darkness. He did not, and spent some difficult moments getting himself back on the bridge before calling for help.

When I told the couple about this incident, they did not comment except to wonder why people hike that late in the day without being more careful. They did think they might know who the guy was. His ways were unusual for Juneau, hair always well trimmed, never out unshaven on a trail or in a store, always wore clean jeans, and had been seen outside of work hours on Sunday wearing a tie. Only legislators do that. With that, I told them that I would see what I could do unofficially and let them know.

Rather than risk making a phone call from home or office or anywhere locally, I volunteered for one of the trips that we occasionally make to Anchorage on police business. Take the early flight up there, do whatever business is needed, have lunch, shop a bit, and try for the 2:30 flight back. I managed to reach corporate headquarters on the first try and was greeted by the automated help menu. After being given numbers to punch for 'Accounting', 'Imports', 'Human Relations', and a string of others, one was finally given one for 'Customer Assistance.' I requested the extension that I had memorized when the case was active. Knowing that the call would be monitored for 'Quality Assurance,' I kept it as brief as possible. I requested that a closed file named 'Zipper' be brought on line. When it had been retrieved, the voice said, "How may I assist you?" I said that I wanted to know what the policy was on returning something about three years old but never used. The voice said, "We can't use it, so we suggest that you keep it or dispose of it. We are willing to reimburse you for so doing. Can I help you with anything else today? No? Have a nice day."

My earlier silent speculation about changing times and political expediencies was now confirmed. Whatever was on the film was no longer of value and could be adverse to company interest in some way. The only logical reason that I could think of was that the political winds were shifting. The country was even more fed up with the male politicians recently seeking office and now, or before too many years, would be seeking a strong and effective female to run. I caught the flight south back to Juneau and was home in time for dinner.

HIDE AND SEEK

My boat rocked gently as I finished reading the journal early in the morning. The sun was starting to come up the channel and over the harbor. Ravens and seagulls were starting their morning raucous litany of nonstop, intermingled bird conversations out on the breakwater. The float was otherwise quiet, though before long the Sunday parade of boats would be heading out for a day of fishing and sunning. As I put the journal down, I realized that I knew who the hunter and the hunted were, subject to doing some further checking 'outside,' which is where you go when you leave Alaska for the lower forty-eight. My conclusions were based on the journal and on some things not in it, but which seemed to dovetail in with it.

Back when I was still among the not yet retired, most radios in Juneau, mine included, would be turned on to the weekday morning show of Chris on KINY as last minute chores were done before heading for work. It's the quick way to get a heads-up on road conditions (rain, snow, ice, the latest accident at the Fred Meyer intersection) and your spot on the birthday list phoned in by people you didn't think knew of it. One sunny morning a caller, who had requested that 'Everywhere you go, sunshine follows you' be played, was chatting with Chris when there was the squawk of a police radio, which was immediately squelched. Chris made some comment about "Did you drop your donut?" and the show went on.

My mind also jumped to a story in the Juneau Empire a year or so earlier about a retired police officer from back east who had joined the Juneau force to fill a spot left vacant by a flood of early retirements. He had also been a guest on KTOO, the local public radio station, to talk about the Child Safety program. The request for the song and the remembered story now led me to paw through the pile of magazines under my galley table for a back issue of Time. It had featured a story on urban legends in America. One of those was about a shadowy figure who seemed to pop up in the news every time a rap star, political figure, world leader or underworld figure died. The person who was healthy was now dead, therefore Sunshine must be involved. He was always thought to be an international assassin responsible even when the death was attributed to natural causes. He had never been seen, or left any trace of foul play, except for the coincidental playing of his theme song just before or after the death.

To be as good as the urban legend claimed, he would have had to possess extraordinary knowledge and talent to do what he was credited with. And not leave any evidence. It was almost as if he had studied for the role.

While I was reading the article, I remembered two of the volunteers who had been fairly regular at our monthly trail workdays. I didn't recall seeing them until a year or two earlier; first they were not on the trail scene, then they were. The couple seemed to have spent a lot of time on the trails and knew a lot of the byways that even some of the old timers were not aware of. Back then, neither of them ever said much, aside from the usual local stuff that was in the paper or soon would be. This is unusual for our town because here almost everyone either works for the city, state or federal government, has done so, plans to do so, or has some family member who does. Everyone knows everyone else or someone else who does. I recalled also that they had mentioned house sitting at one time. Were they the couple being chased? One thing for sure was that I would not bring the subject up while standing near the Glory Hole.

Before trying to get a few hours of sleep, I carefully placed the journal in several layers of plastic freezer bags and used the Alaska universal sealer, also known as duct tape, to further secure it. I stuffed it under my blankets between me and the bulkhead and managed to sleep for a couple of hours. Then, at mid-day, when I could best watch for watchers, I thought of a short-term hiding place for the journal.

The place that I decided on was one that I had walked over for years without even realizing that it was there. It doesn't even show up on my boat plans. I only discovered it by chance one winter when I left town on business and asked a friend to check the boat to be sure the water system didn't freeze up. He didn't and it did. When I got back and thawed the pipes out, the fresh water pump cycled off and on more than normal. I could also hear the faint sound of escaping water near the amidships galley sink. The water lines to the sink were gray PVC that ran down inside the hull and disappeared under the cabin floor.

Then the pipes somehow managed to snake inboard and forward coming out of a tunnel with various wires and control cables in the hold (basement?) under the wheelhouse to join the rest of the plumbing. Back upstairs, after lifting the galley carpet off the tack strips, I studied the old vinyl floor covering. There were faint impressions of screw heads under the vinyl. After lifting the vinyl in the amidships area, I was able to unscrew and lift a section of flooring two feet long and six inches wide. The damaged pipe branched off from a maze of wires, cables, and tubes running along the narrow tunnel. I replaced the leaking pipe and was back in business.

Now I returned to that spot and was able to fit the package in under the floorboards and outboard of the tunnel wall between the deck and the hull. Before I screwed the board back down and put the carpet back on the tack strips, I jury-rigged a switch that would be tripped if the board was tampered with. If the board was lifted, the boat horn would start bleating and perhaps alert my neighbors.

Later, I walked down to the main float, past the *Relentless*, and up to the pay phone at the top of the ramp. From there I could see my boat and also the *Relentless*, which appeared to be empty. I booked an Alaska Airlines flight to San Diego to go and try to confirm my conclusions. After that I walked back down to my boat and spent the afternoon doing some digging around in the 'archives' stored on board. The couple had not identified Ernie except by first name, that he was an attorney, and that he shared a family name with one of the older and more prestigious law firms in San Diego. Having spent a few years in San Diego doing legal work at the other end of the scale gave me at least a start on finding him.

One of the lesser reasons that I moved to Alaska as a single person is my tendency to save things that I might need or have use for some time in the future. My former wife saw it as being a packrat; I saw it as being prudent. This time, being prudent won. I went forward to the wheel-house / living room / TV room / lounge / computer room and lifted the lid / hatch that accesses the basement / hold where the fuel tanks, water heater, non-functioning furnace, and bilge pump are housed. It is also an on-board storage area for the things that have overflowed from my storage locker on shore.

After rearranging some of the stacks and riffling through several unlabeled boxes, I finally found one that had stuff from when I had dreams of being the next F. Lee Bailey or Perry Mason. There, just where I had left it in case it was ever needed, was a directory of attorneys in the San Diego County Bar Association. The directory had what were essentially high-class mug shots of most of the over three thousand attorneys that I had been in competition with. The listings also gave office information, affiliation if any, and law school attended. I was pictured with more hair and no beard.

After finding the historical document and returning to the main deck level, I spent several hours looking for a crossover of names of the major firms to smaller firms or sole practitioners. I tried to narrow the choices down to those with the correct first name or to those using the initial E. It would have been easier if it was not for the rampant overuse of first initial, middle name followed by last name affectations. After a lot of time spent squinting at the small black and white squares, I finally found one that seemed to fit.

I called information to see if there was a home phone listed. There was. The address listed was out in one of the better areas right on the beach. I was almost sure that I had the right person. Still, my cards might not be enough to make him respond openly.

I returned the directory to the hold, packed, and was on my way early the next morning. Knowing that such directness might raise a flag to those folks now apparently interested in me, I became a typical San Diego tourist, walked beaches, visited old friends, dined well, read the legal newspapers for court calendars, and bided my time. I drove past the address I had for Ernie and saw an older green Blazer in the driveway. I also checked the latest attorney directory for a better picture of Ernie. I spent some time at the courthouse wandering the halls remembering the victories and the more common setbacks, happy to not be a part of the scene. A whole new generation of eager young hotshots roamed the halls seeking glory in the form of big paydays.

Then one day I managed to pass Ernie as he was checking the court calendar outside Department 34 of the Superior Court. I started to read the same board and said in a low voice, "Your two friends said to say hello from the Last Frontier. I'll be in the attorney lounge in fifteen minutes." I walked down the hall to the next courtroom, went in, and sat for a few minutes. Then I left, took the stairs up to the next floor, and entered the room through a door marked 'Attorney's Lounge' - no double meaning, I hoped.

The room was empty except for me when Ernie walked in a few minutes later with another attorney. They talked briefly and the other attorney left. He turned to me and said "Explain that message."

I said "Show me your bar card."

He quickly produced cards showing state and local bar membership. He was apparently the lawyer mentioned in the journal. Then I said, "I'm from Alaska. I hike a lot. I was in a very remote shelter and found a journal intended to answer questions some children might have. Your first name was mentioned. I think that I know the couple in the journal and also who is still looking for them."

His expression did not change. I said, "They are safe for now. But whatever you do to check me out, don't contact the local or state police up there. That could put them and me in danger." As I said that, I handed him a slip of paper with my name and post office box number and suggested that he run my name past the California State Bar roster.

He said only, "Nice meeting you, have a safe trip." and left the room quickly. After waiting a few minutes, I left, took the stairs to the second floor, spent some time in the clerk's office, and then headed outside and over to Broadway. As I headed back to my motel, I realized that the fact that he had not blustered or denied but said nothing seemed to be the confirmation that I was seeking.

Early the next morning, I checked out of the motel, turned in my car, and caught the city bus downtown. After some breakfast at the IHOP near the courthouse, I headed west on Broadway. My soft-sided briefcase contained, among my souvenirs, a change of socks and underwear and my shaving gear. My main suitcase was waiting for a FedEx pickup back at the motel, where it would appear that I would return for it. By 9:30 I was on the Amtrak shuttle headed to Los Angeles. As far as I could tell, I was the last person to board - but what about the stops along the way? I guess you just do what you can to CYA.

In Los Angeles, I left the train station, walked to the Olivera Street area, had lunch outside, and strolled toward the downtown area. If I was being followed, they were good at keeping out of sight. I passed the bus terminal, circled the block, went in, and bought a ticket for Seattle. As I went toward the boarding area, I watched two guys in suits question the agent, then pass the place I was watching from. As the bus pulled out with the two guys on board, I put on a cap and dark glasses and returned to the ticket area. I went to a different window and bought a ticket for Omaha. The bus left in twenty minutes. My trackers were hopefully on the way to Seattle.

Three days later, after sampling bus station food of every quality level, mostly not haute cuisine, I was in New York City somewhat weary and wanting a bed to sleep in. I found a small hotel that was reluctantly willing to accept cash rather than a credit card, showered for a long time after blocking the room door with a chair, and slept like one can only do after being on a bus across the country. The next day, I called FedEx and arranged for them to pick up my bag. I hoped that it wasn't being tracked by anyone except FedEx.

I managed to find my way over to New Jersey later in the day. After arriving in the city mentioned in the Juneau newspaper article a year earlier, I went to the local newspaper and settled in for a search of their files. It didn't take long, though, to find what I wanted as I had a name to start with. And there it was. Lots of stories about the local cop hero, retired after twenty years, clean record i.e. never on the take, family man, involved in volunteer activities, enjoyed traveling, intended to do some PI work and consulting after retirement.

On a sudden hunch, I called the newsroom and managed to talk to the police beat reporter. I ask if the retiree was still doing PI work. His answer filled in the blanks as he said, "Not any more. His wife was staying home to care for her parents and work while he traveled. Then suddenly about a year ago he moved her and him lock, stock, and barrel to a new cop shop job somewhere in the frozen north. If that don't beat all."

"Did you know him?", was my next question.

"Know him?", he replied in a voice that seemed to reek of cigarettes and alcohol and years of writing about people mostly at very low levels. "I knew Jimmy D. from the day that he graduated from the academy and was sworn in as a rookie cop. It was about the time I started as a reporter for this rag. There was some mention at the ceremony about him carrying on the family tradition, his dad and granddad also being cops. Our careers sort of went along side by side till he retired at twenty years. He had a reputation for being a totally honest cop, never used a day of sick leave when he wasn't sick, a real family man, and never let fear keep him from doing what he had to do."

"Me, I covered what I call the crime and punishment beat, still do, while he went up the ladder to be head of the detective bureau. Nothing ever seemed to faze him, even that one time early on. He was the first guy to arrive at a 'shots fired' call at an abandoned warehouse out in the industrial area. I had heard the dispatch on the scanner and got there almost as quick as he did. He entered the building just as his backup pulled up. Light from the dirty overhead windows showed a surreal scene neither of us will ever forget. Six bodies were laid out in a row, blood was everywhere and the stench was overpowering. It wasn't only so much that each guy had died from a pistol shot to the back of the head gangland style, it was that afterwards they had all been decapitated - arms and legs cut off by automatic weapons fire.

"One of them was Jimmy D's high school buddy who had tried to get on the force and didn't make it. I remember to this day how Jimmy D. bent over, threw up, wiped his mouth, cried, and crossed himself. Then he stood up, identified the body, and went on with his job. I think that was when his career started to take off."

I thanked him for his time and headed for the airport.

HELP WANTED

My secret Secret Service agent role seemed to be going nowhere even faster. Since my less than successful effort to hike with the couple who I thought might be the people I was looking for, I had hiked less while recovering from my ankle injury. I thought back to the hikes they had been part of, and what clues I might have missed about them. The husband worked for the state in some type of contract review role for the Department of Administration. The wife worked at the city library downtown and had been a big help in finding material for the mining history research I had been doing.

While they were of an age to have kids in college or out on their own, I didn't recall any mention of them having children or grandchildren. Just a pleasant couple who showed up on a regular basis for the hikes, joined in the conversations along the way, and seemed, well, average. They did not have a phone number listed, which is not unusual, so no home address was listed either. They drove different cars from time to time which doesn't prove anything. Their history locally was hard to figure without seeming nosy. People do arrive here, take state jobs, and don't always discuss their past in detail.

If I had access to driver's license information, maybe I could have figured out when they got up here. Calling the employer to learn a date of hire might get back to them and alert them somehow.

For now I was reduced to casually observing and wondering about them.

Then I finally got a break when I was driving out Thane Road one morning to take pictures of some relics that were not too far from the road. When I passed the Sheep Creek Trailhead, I saw a car pulled off in the parking area. The couple I wondered about was unloading backpacks from the trunk and looked like they were heading out to stay a while. I didn't stop to ask questions because that might be obvious, and also I didn't want to risk another injury.

When I finished taking the pictures I had planned out toward the DuPont Trailhead, I headed back toward town. The car they had been unloading from was no longer at the Sheep Creek Trailhead. I pulled into the parking area and started to get my pack out as if I planned to hike up the trail. It didn't take much looking to find their packs hidden in the underbrush near the trail.

I left, drove into town to have coffee at Valentine's, and returned to the trailhead two hours later. Their packs were gone and there was no car parked there. My next stop was the library, where I asked one of the staff if Anne would be in today as she was trying to locate a book for me. She said that Anne had a sudden family emergency and would not be in for a while. The couple missed the Saturday hike also, but when I went to the library three days later, there she was as cheerful as ever and made no mention of an emergency.

On the Saturday hike that weekend, a couple of the guys who volunteer to help maintain the local trails were talking about an offer the Forest Service had made to take over some shelters up past the end of the Sheep Creek Trail. The guys were planning to hike up that direction to scope out the trail and the shelters to see what might be involved in using them in some way.

The two events made me think that maybe the area up the Sheep Creek Trail should be checked out. Maybe the film was stashed up there somewhere as it had not been found anyplace else. That's when I called for help, as this was my first real lead in nearly three years. Maybe the agents in the Lower 48 weren't too busy at that time, as help arrived in a matter of days by air and by sea in the form of a helicopter and a cabin cruiser. I didn't know that the Secret Service had that type of resources, but maybe someone with clout finally realized that help would be nice. Or perhaps other buttons were being pushed to get the matter resolved before the administration left office.

The fact is that with the helicopter people and the boat people showing up, I was also 'blessed' with the arrival of the person responsible for me being here for so long. He had retired, but for reasons not stated had decided to come up here and look around. After calling to say hello, meeting for coffee, and questions about how are you enjoying your assignment?, he was off being a tourist. We didn't discuss my assignment, except for me saying that I had made no real progress other than sighting a lot of couples who might be the ones. Maybe I did mention my accident and who I was following when it happened.

But, again, even with the extra help, my timing was slightly off. The trail group went up to look at the shelters the same day that my reinforcements arrived to help me. I didn't try to go with the team that headed up to the shelters as I was still staying under my cover. Because of the short time available to prepare for the hike, there was not a lot of time to brief the new people on how the locals dress. Any local hikers seeing them move up the trail would certainly have wondered where these guys in designer hiking gear dropped in from. They looked like an ad from an Eddie Bauer catalog.

The team did make it up to the shelters after passing the trail people on their way back down. An earlier report from the helicopter had let them know that there was no indication of anything being found; at least no open display of anything being passed around. How much can you tell from a helicopter anyway? If something had been there, it was gone now. One of the boards on the shelter floor had been recently broken, but it was not possible to tell if something had been hidden under it. We decided to watch the hikers come and go for a few days to see if anything unusual resulted.

The cruiser that some of the team showed up on had tied up at the transient moorage in the harbor just a short distance away from one of the trail guys who lives on a boat. That was a good move because that one was off on an Alaska Airlines flight headed for San Diego a day or so later. All of this, while interesting, took precious time away from my research at a critical time when my book project was almost done.

Then, as quickly as they had arrived, the helicopter and the cruiser departed, taking my helpers with them. I had started to get back to my regular routines when another interruption occurred. I had pulled in to park at the downtown library on the lower level where spots are reserved for library users. My plan was to spend a few hours checking some reference material so that I could finish my book.

As I got out of my wagon, a police car pulled up beside me. I recognized the officer from some of our Saturday hikes and his help in getting me off the bridge when I injured myself. He chatted for a few minutes, asked how my ankle was, and commented on how amazing it was that my rustmobile was still going. Then he said, "There is a small meeting being set up in a room at the Emporium Mall next week. That couple that we know from the Saturday hikes will be there. There will also be an officer from the San Diego Police Department. It's very informal, but you might want to listen in." He said nothing about the agency I work for as he gave me the time and place of the meeting and drove off. I decided it might be smart for me to attend the meeting just in case it answered any questions for me. It might also allow me to come out of exile.

THE UMBRELLA MAN

Summer started to wind down accompanied by the annual appearance of fireweed. We awoke one Saturday morning to a non-sound. After a brief time of confusion, we realized that the rains of the past weeks had stopped. To our further surprise, the sun was out and the sky was a vivid blue. A day such as this one promised to be is rare in Juneau, and even rarer on a Saturday. It's the kind of day when things like work, shopping, and even doctor appointments are immediately rearranged, and fishing, hiking or driving somewhere without the wipers on takes priority.

We immediately decided to head into town for breakfast at Bacar's on Franklin before heading for a hike on the Mt. Roberts Trail. The plan was to see whether the local trail group had dealt with the mud on the lower part of the trail, maybe hike on up to the cross at the top of Mt. Roberts before having a late lunch at the restaurant in the tram terminal building, and then ride the tram down in time to find a place to fish on the way home if the rains had not returned.

Without any further thought about grocery shopping or other usual weekend rituals, we dressed in jeans, flannel shirts and vests and pulled on the rubber boots known locally as Juneau tennies. We loaded coffee cups to hold us while we headed into town, grabbed our backpacks, and were off to savor the day. After a leisurely breakfast, and more coffee at the restaurant under the American Legion Post downtown, we walked up the street to Fifth and headed for the trailhead between the houses at the edge of the city. We climbed the steel steps past the porches bordering the trail and headed for the first of many switchbacks. Except for the switchbacks, the trail is all uphill and offers occasional great views of the city one way and Silverbow Basin the other way. An hour or so later we were at the tram terminal area and still had time to hike up to the cross before stopping for lunch.

Perhaps the brightness of the day lulled us into being less careful than usual. No one was aware of our last minute plans, and no one had passed us as we hiked up the trail. By now, we should have given more thought to the idea that pursuers don't always have to follow; it is also easy to just wait at a known point. Such as around a place like the tram terminal. But it was a glorious day and we were enjoying ourselves. After lunch and a few minutes' wait while Mom toured the gift shop, we walked outside and over to the nature shop run by Gastineau Guiding. Then as we returned to the terminal, we saw the police officer we had talked to about our plan. He was not in uniform and was talking with one of the tram supervisors. He nodded to us as we entered the building and headed up the stairs to the loading area.

By the time we joined the crowd of tourists waiting to board the Raven car for the downward trip, the officer was also in the crowd. The tourists were easy to identify as they wore the light plastic raingear issued by the cruise lines even though it was not raining. In Juneau, when it is not raining, it soon will be. Most of them also carried at least one of the standard issue cruise line umbrellas. They seemed to be the usual elderly or older couples who make up the majority of the summer visitors, although there was one well-dressed man who seemed to be traveling alone. He was wearing the L.L. Bean/Eddie Bauer type of gear and Danner boots, as compared to the blue jeans and rubber boots most of us locals seem to favor for practical reasons. Somehow he had managed to avoid getting mud on his boots, which might have set a local record.

We pressed forward with the crowd and boarded the car. As the sliding doors of the tram car closed and the boarding ramps raised, the car moved quickly away from the platform and headed down toward the city below. The car was crowded with tourists, a few tram employees and some other hikers. The mudless man had taken a spot a few steps from where we were at the front of the car. There was a lot of chatter as the car passed over the trees that had been trimmed when the cable was hung a few years earlier. Everything seemed normal as we waited for our favorite view of the channel and the harbor. It had been a perfect day.

As we were nearing the halfway point on the descent, where cameras were out and clicking away as we passed the up car on the other cable, the mudless male passenger suddenly seemed to lose his balance and lurched toward me. While he tried to regain his footing, his umbrella raised slightly and almost poked me in the leg. As it came level, I saw the policeman step forward, grab the man's wrist, and force the umbrella downward as he helped the man regain his balance. The officer must have had a very strong grip, because I saw the man grimace in pain before the officer released his hold. For an instant the guy looked exactly like I do when hit with a flu shot needle. The brief commotion didn't seem to faze the other passengers, who were watching the harbor scene below and trying to take pictures while the car continued down.

Soon Raven was docking at the lower terminal. As the platform lowered and the doors slid open, the tourists rushed out to head back for their ships or to do more shopping and take another tour. The officer seemed to be intent on watching the departing umbrella man. As I thanked him for helping keep me from being poked with an umbrella, he said quietly, "Your history lesson for today is on the life and death of Georgi Markov. Have a nice day."

With that he walked away. We were baffled by his words as we walked out of the terminal and headed toward downtown. Why would he be giving us a history lesson? Still, being curious about the officer's comment, we stopped at the library a few blocks away and did some quick computer research that brought us a chilling blast of reality. We all live with the remote, but ever lurking knowledge, that our earthly journey can be ended in an instant. The oncoming car that crosses the center line, a loose engine from the airplane five miles overhead, or from some body function that goes askew without warning. In our exile, an added element of danger was always carried with us. Now a new form of it had crossed the center line and just missed us.

Georgi Markov was not hard to find with an online search. He was a Bulgarian novelist and playwright who defected to the West in 1969. During his exile, his many broadcasts for Radio Free Europe did not endear him to the communist rulers in his homeland. In 1978, while walking to his office in London, a man carrying an umbrella bumped into him. Markov died after three days of agony from the effects of a usually untraceable poison injected by a pellet fired from the tip of the umbrella. If the tiny pellet had dissolved as planned, the cause of his death might never have been known. The research also taught us a new word - one that again increased our awareness of the narrow path we traveled. Ricin had never been in our vocabulary before. It is a biotoxin possibly much more lethal than cobra venom and leaves no trace. We now try to avoid places where people carry umbrellas. Which is hard to do most of the time in Juneau.

HEADLINE - THE JUNEAU EMPIRE:

TOURIST DEATH BAFFLES DOCTORS

The sudden unexplained death of an apparently healthy tourist continues to baffle doctors at Bartlett Memorial Hospital and at the state medical laboratory in Anchorage.

Geoffrey M. Hightower of Andover, Maryland was in Juneau on an independent tour of Alaska. He was staying at the Baranoff Hotel and had been seen last Saturday in the area of the Mt. Roberts Tram Upper Terminal. He apparently became ill while walking back to the hotel from the lower terminal. He collapsed as he entered the hotel lobby at about 4 p.m. Paramedics from the Juneau Fire Department were called and rushed him to the hospital, where he died early Monday morning.

He was treated for a high fever and possible blood poisoning of undetermined origin, possibly causing kidney failure. There was no indication of an accident causing any injury to Mr. Hightower except for a minor puncture wound on one leg. An autopsy is pending in Anchorage.

Family members who were contacted stated that he had no known health problems and had passed a routine physical examination shortly before his trip. Mr. Hightower was a retired federal employee and leaves a wife and two adult children.

BACK TO MY FLOATING HOME

I got back from my excursion around the Lower 48 on the Alaska Airlines afternoon milk run out of Seattle. The long trip had confirmed who at least some of the players were, but didn't give me a clue as to what I could or should do next. The only thing that I was sure of was that the couple was still living in Juneau in plain sight. And that the shadowy urban legend called Sunshine was apparently also there in plain sight. Yet if he had located his targets, why had he not taken some action?

Then, also, logic would indicate that someone had to be hanging around for the feds - a Secret Service agent perhaps. If I had to cast someone in that role, it would be the guy taking endless pictures of mining relics. Some of us were still laughing about the time on the Treadwell Mining Area Trail when he was taking pictures of some scrap iron near where the trail heads toward the beach and the old buildings. After he had finished his shots, we pointed out that the scrap had molded letters spelling out GM POWERGLIDE and maybe was not from the mining era.

Anyway, if the parties were who I thought, what next? I certainly was not going to ask the officer if he was also known as Sunshine or the couple if they had hidden a journal in a shelter up on the ridge. Or had a roll of film found in San Diego.

After my flight landed, I caught a ride to the boat harbor with some friends and walked down the ramp toward my boat. As I got to the main float at the bottom of the ramp, the couple living across the water from me on a retired workboat over on C float were headed for the ramp up to the parking lot. They greeted me and asked how my trip was. Then they thanked me for waking them up. I asked how I could do that if I wasn't there.

They said that on the night I left, the horn on my boat had started blasting about 3 a.m. The man, being 'older,' had gotten up to use his marine head. Knowing him, he had probably just walked out to the stern. He was headed back to bed when it all started. As my boat horn blasted away, he quickly stepped out onto the stern of their boat and saw two people jump off of my boat, apparently in a huge hurry and headed toward the main float. But he didn't see them go up the lighted ramp, which was visible from his boat. By then his wife was awake and they threw on their clothes and went over to my boat. The padlock on my door had been cut and it appeared that someone had been inside looking for something.

He had found the electrical panel and pulled a fuse to shut the horn off. They looked around and saw that the usual things that would be stolen, like electronic gear and fishing tackle, had not been bothered. The carpet in the main area had been lifted and the hatch to the storage area was raised. They replaced the cut lock with one of theirs and left the interior lights on when they left. The next morning, the Relentless had left and headed down the channel.

I assured my friends that I didn't have anything on board that justified a search. Maybe it was just someone wanting to see the inside of a real houseboat. Why cut a lock though? Many curious dock walkers do peer into boat windows, but not usually at 3 a.m. They gave me the key to the new padlock. I thanked them for their help and they went on up the ramp. I went on down to my boat, got on board, and found that most everything was intact. Some things were moved, but with my housekeeping, who could really tell? In some ways it was neater than when I had left. One screw had been loosened in the floorboards, which had caused the contact on my jury-rigged alarm to break and set off the horn. Primitive but effective anyway. At least the journal was right where I had left it.

While I continued to ponder about what I could or should do, the solution, a decision by delay, arrived a few days later with no effort on my part. I had driven downtown to pick up some special blend coffee at the Heritage Coffee Shop in the Emporium Mall. After parking on Shattuck Way in back of City Hall, rather than trying to find a place on Franklin Street, I went in by the rear entrance. As I walked in, a police officer I recognized and had recently been checking on was also walking in. We said hello and he headed for the steps to the second floor as I headed down the hall toward the coffee place.

I had turned from the counter with the coffee that I had bought when I saw the couple I had also been checking on enter the mall and take the front steps to the second floor. While I was wondering about the coincidence of the officer also being up there, there was another one. The relic photographer came in, followed by a man dressed in slacks, sport jacket, white shirt, tie, and loafers. It was not quite the typical Juneau dress code for a time when the legislature is not in session. The guy walked like a movie cop in civilian clothes. He also headed up the stairs.

I took my coffee and wandered down the hall to window shop and look at the pictures of old Juneau on the walls. That's how a few minutes later I saw a parade of all the parties come down the rear stairs, enter the photo shop next to the rear entrance (had this drama gone full circle?), and go around the counter into the work area. It seemed like a good time to get a cup of coffee to sip and to watch for what happened next.

About an hour later, the events were played in reverse. The various people came out of the work area, around the counter, out of the shop, and headed back upstairs. They seemed subdued and were not chattering. After another fifteen minutes, the people came back down the stairs and left the same way they had arrived. The possible Secret Service guy was offering the guy in sport jacket and loafers a ride to the airport. What had happened upstairs that might have to do with the journal?

Now that the parade had ended, I went to the photo shop to see if some of my prints were ready. The clerk asked if I could wait a few minutes because they were running behind as their machine had been being used for police business. So perhaps this was the end of the journey and the journal end might never be written. Regardless, there were some unresolved questions.

Such as what to do with the journal, if anything? What should I do about knowing who Sunshine is? Knowing of his reputation concerned me most. Did he know or even suspect that his cover was gone? It was not something I planned to ask him about the next time he joined us on a hike. As a matter of fact, I didn't plan to tell the couple that I had their journal. Maybe I would mail it to the attorney in San Diego or put it back where I had found it - but what if someone else found it? Perhaps those sleeping dogs had best not be annoyed.

Sunshine - An Informal Meeting

While I was doing the groundwork for closing 'Zipper' once and for all, I managed to keep watch on the couple so that nothing would happen to them before the film was finally recovered. There had been the matter of the wild card retired federal employee who I had spotted downtown one day. Maybe it was a matter of 'takes one to know one' that made me wonder if he really was a casual tourist. Some people blend in so well that they stand out. Or maybe it was his wearing the shades even when they weren't needed. He also seemed to be where my new friends were too many times to be mere happenstance.

I watched and waited till he took a tram ride one day when I knew they had left to hike up the Mt. Roberts Trail. After what happened on the tram, I could only hope that their combined math skills would not allow them to factor in what I had said to them into any conclusion that I was anything other than a friendly local cop helping them solve a personal problem.

My first move to solve that problem had been to contact the lieutenant at the San Diego Police Department to tell him that I had located the couple he wanted to talk to. Could he arrange to fly up and meet with them? He said that the murder they had stumbled onto was still quite unsolved. Talking to them might at least fill in some of the blanks. I suggested that he plan to come up as soon as I had arranged things with the other folks involved.

The Secret Service guy who was finishing his third year here had put in for retirement and would probably be leaving here soon, though by now he was an authority on the local trails. He had never officially admitted why he was here, other than to say he was doing advance work for the next time the President came to Juneau. As no one here can remember the last time that happened, his work seemed less than necessary. I did not want to use the word 'boondoggle.' His actual purpose here was probably to ride herd on the couple to be sure that, if he ever found them, they didn't try to use the film, and also to see who else might be after it.

I was aware that he had recently been joined by several other agents for a few days. Maybe the President was planning a trip here and would be hiking the Sheep Creek Trail. The trio had gone hiking in that area and later were seen motoring around the harbor in a cabin cruiser with an Oregon name on the stern. That might have something to do with the helicopter that arrived at the airport about that time, flew around a few times, and left as mysteriously as it had arrived.

When the ducks were all in a row, I arranged for a meeting in a vacant room above the Heritage Coffee Shop in the Emporium Mall on South Franklin Street. This offered some privacy in that people could enter from the street or from Shattuck Way behind City Hall. The place also allowed access to a photo shop where I had arranged to develop the film. I hoped that part would not be too traumatic for the couple after what had happened the last time they ventured into one. The idea was to develop the film, maybe make a set of prints, and then take everything back to our meeting place. This was to ensure what lawyers refer to as 'chain of custody' with no possible bootleg copies. After seeing what was on the film, everything would be destroyed except our memories and we would, as the Bible says, 'go in peace.'

At the time and place we had agreed on, the couple arrived and came up the front stairs of the mall. They gave their local names of Hal and Anne, which all of us realized didn't match the ones on the rental agreement for the car in San Diego. Hal said simply that they had been in San Diego several years earlier, found a roll of film in a rental car, and brought the film to Juneau with them. There was a possibility that the film was related to some things that had happened in San Diego. Now they wanted to turn it in with the hope that anyone looking for it would stop looking for them. If not, so be it. They were ready to take their chances.

The Secret Service guy, sensing that his record length assignment might finely end, agreed that his agency would make contact with the group that originally placed the order for the pictures so that they would know that the film had been found and destroyed. With that the suspense as to whether the film had actually been brought to the meeting and where it had been for the past three years came full circle. I, in my former role, had searched diligently for it and never found a trace of where it might be hidden. There, to my knowledge, was no secret safe deposit box, hidden compartment in a kitchen junk drawer, or in a cookie jar or under flour or sugar. Somehow, they had managed to keep it hidden from people who make a living finding what can't be found. We almost needed a drum roll as Hal said, "We know we have been found and identified, tracked, followed, and had our homes and cars searched. We have been watched as we shopped, hiked, set, stood, and lord knows what else. Even as we took pictures, we have been watched. Yet, thanks to my common sense wife, what is the common denominator in all that?"

My mind raced to the too obvious conclusion even faster then the Secret Service guy who looked like a light bulb had finally flashed on in his head and it hurt.

With that Anne reached into her backpack and brought out the camera some of us had seen them use over the years. She opened it, took out the roll of film from it, and said, "When hiding cookies, chocolate chips or kisses from kids or spouse, the obvious hiding place is the best. It's even better if the hiding place can be taken with you. This camera has been taken out, turned on, focused, snapped, and turned off hundreds of times over the past three years. The film never advanced because it wasn't threaded in this camera as it had already been exposed when we found it. We have another camera we use for really taking pictures."

With that, she took out the film and handed it to me. We all stood up and walked downstairs to the backroom of the photo shop to watch as the film was developed and printed. The technician had set the process in motion and left the room as we huddled around the machine in silent anticipation. When the prints emerged one after the other, our speculations about what might have happened in

San Diego became living color reality. Two of the people on the prints were easy to recognize: our soon to be former commander in chief with a startled look on his face, and our local Secret Service agent. There was also a lady sitting on the couch with her skirt pulled open except that some of the shots showed that she was he. The later shots showed a look of puzzlement on the President's face as he had turned to say something to the agent. The last shots, less in focus, showed the agent escorting the lady from the room.

The area around the machine was silent for a moment, perhaps because of what was on the prints, perhaps because of a realization that we were seeing what had happened on that long ago night which had led to the entire domino effect, had such repercussions, and had been now best be put to rest. We took the prints and the negatives and walked in silence back upstairs. When we were back behind the closed door, the Secret Service agent spoke first. "The code words that night were 'Silence is golden.' We will never acknowledge, comment on, or in any way say anything about this. There will be an out agency call to a group we interface with, and won't ever confirm working with, that 'Operation Zipper' is now closed."

The San Diego police lieutenant said, "Our files on the photo shop case and the drowning at the airport will remain unsolved but inactive. If we ever develop (no pun intended) any leads on the case of the woman/man in the dumpster, our focus will be on what happened in the alley adjacent to the hotel, nothing else. With that, the Juneau police officer burned the negatives and prints in a wastebasket before flushing the ashes down the toilet in a backroom. Maybe that final step made things come full circle for the photographer.

With our business completed, bonds forever but never to be revealed, we went our separate ways. The couple left carrying a now empty camera. I headed to the station to supervise shift change, and the Secret Service guy left to pack for his return south. He also had to attend a brief memorial service for a guy he had once worked with who had died while visiting up here. I didn't comment on that or on the swarm of agents who had come and gone from our town recently. The San Diego Police guy had to catch a flight north to Anchorage to meet his wife, who was busy shopping there to get more airline miles.

The next morning was a sunny day and KINY was again playing 'Everywhere you go, sunshine follows you.'

WHAT NEXT?

Mom and I left the Mall and turned left on Franklin Street heading for where we had parked an hour or so earlier. Some phone calls needed to be made before too long. A flood of tourists just off a cruise ship surrounded us as we walked in silence. In some ways it was reminiscent of the crowds on that evening in San Diego when we fled to the Old Town area. Each time, decisions had to be made that could lead us down various unknown paths. And each time we were surrounded by hurrying people who probably could not imagine what we had just gone through.

Somehow we didn't get to the car, but found ourselves headed up Franklin toward Fernando's for an early dinner while we continued to silently ponder our fate. Our friend, the owner, greeted us in his usual outgoing way as we made our way back to a table at the rear of the dining area. He brought us two cold bottles of Negra Modelo with chilled glasses and asked if we wanted our usual order. After we said, "Yes," he left for the kitchen. As we sat, Mom led off with her thoughts.

Her candid opinion was that something as simple as what we had just seen should not have cost us all that it had. Three years out of our lives away from our family just because some bozo couldn't keep his hands in his pockets. We could have been killed and no one would ever have known why. She was just hitting full stride with her thoughts as our dinners and another round of beer arrived. Before she could launch into another tirade, I managed to remind her that there had been some other considerations in our decision to duck for cover. That steered her away from the verbal assault on certain men who can't resist chasing every skirt in sight and diverted her to thoughts on what was next for us.

"In a way," she said, "we started a new life together when we were on that deck in San Diego. Up till then it had been you, me, and the kids in an almost ideal world. A whole chunk of your buried past was with you, but not with us. Somehow, we came here even more together than we had been before. Maybe we should go forward together where we are rather than try to return to life as it was."

What she said made a lot of sense to me. Our life before had been good and normal and would have led to eventual retirement, maybe in a warmer climate where kids and grandkids could come to visit. Now, in a way, we had seen the other side of the mountain. There were other lives to be lived, other people to meet, trails to be tried. So I cautiously asked, "What do you have in mind?"

Apparently she had done a lot of her thinking before the meeting, as she quickly replied, "I say we stay here. You have enough years in to retire from where you were working. The kids are almost out of school and they don't need a family home to keep them from heading out on their own. We can sell the house and buy a smaller one here so we won't be packing every two or three months. And we can buy a car that has real air conditioning, not just from having a Juneau body."

I have learned from being married to your mom for over twenty years that her opinions are always very well thought out and make enough sense to be agreed with. I would make some token objections for the record before we did exactly as she had suggested. It would be a lot easier to go forward from where we were than try to answer questions from former neighbors about how our trip had been. If they only knew.

With our future decided on, we finished our dinners, paid the check, said good night to our host, and headed across the street to the Baranof to make some phone calls from their lobby. The first one was to our number back where we had left for a month's vacation three years earlier. The phone rang but no one answered. Why weren't the boys there waiting for our call; they should have known that sooner or later we would be calling? I left a message that we were coming in from the cold and would try again later.

Then I placed a call to Ernie to let him know that the plan we had discussed with him had worked out and that we were deciding what to do now that the heat was off. I also told him that it had been so cold here last winter that a local attorney had been seen with his hands in his own pockets. He laughed and said, "While you are telling jokes from the Attorney's Handbook, you should be on the road to the airport to meet a couple of people." With that he laughed and hung up.

Not sure of what he was talking about, but hoping that we had figured it out, we hurried to the car and headed out Egan Drive toward the airport. As we drove, an Alaska flight was headed south out over Douglas Island before making the turn to land.

We parked as the plane was headed for the terminal and were upstairs as the passengers started coming down the ramp. We saw a lot of people we had met over the years here, but only three we had known before. No wonder they had not answered the phone. And of course Mom was beside herself with questions about who was taking care of what while they were gone and was Kevin on leave? It was the best reunion possible with Mom setting a record for tissue crumpling. There was even time for a quick tour around town before the sunset. After that, on to our current house, where we sat in front of the fire and started catching up.

The catching up was aided by a package we found in the car as the boys climbed in when we left the airport. How it got from the shelter to the car was a question to file, along with how the items from the coroner's office got to us three years earlier.

After seeing the upstairs-downstairs-upstairs-downstairs scene at the Emporium Mall where the various players apparently met, conferred, and left in peace, I took the coffee I had bought and returned to my boat to think about life, people, and what the hell I should do. I had a whole bunch of conclusions and a journal that added up to a very warm potato that I didn't want to deal with.

Then I remembered the point in the journal when Anne had asked "Do we need an attorney?" Maybe I needed one. So I called the same one they had called and caught him at home. He listened without comment as I told him of what I had seen today and what I had concluded earlier. His suggestion was that if I was right it might not be a good idea to make my thoughts known outside of what now was covered by attorney/client confidentiality. He also said that if I hurried I might see a car being parked at the airport and it might be an opportune time to return something I had found without a lot of questions being asked. And that his bill for the consultation would take into consideration that the services were outside of office hours. I thanked him and hung up as I left for the airport.

When the couple and the three boys joined the rest of us on the Saturday hike, I just greeted them as usual. I did mention to the group that our relic photographer was headed for Colorado and ruins there, after attending a memorial service for a guy he had worked with outside who had died while visiting Juneau. I also announced that our policeman hiker couldn't join us as his wife needed his help in running a quilt show. So let's head out and see what the new cabin at Windfall Lake looks like.

Several months later the Saturday hikers were among the guests invited to a housewarming at Hal and Anne's new home. It's over on Douglas Island on Blueberry Hill overlooking the channel and Juneau. Several trailheads were within a short walk. I was enjoying the view while chatting with friends when our host introduced me to a guest from out of town. I felt it best not to say that I had met the visitor earlier on a trip to San Diego.

Ernie also apparently felt it wise not to say anything about our prior conversations. He did express surprise that anyone who had ever lived in San Diego could find happiness anywhere else. When our host drifted off to greet other guests, Ernie and I took our beers and stepped out onto the deck. We hit it off right away as I told him about the local attorney who was seen downtown with a pig under his arm. Someone came along and asked, "Where did you get him?" The pig replied, "I won him at a raffle."

Then I asked if he could tell me what he was doing here. He said he was working under the Alaska Attorneys Full Employment Act. That's a rule that allows an out-of-state attorney to practice in Alaska without being licensed in Alaska - as long as an Alaska attorney is with him. That way both can bill the client.

Then he said, "You can probably imagine that there are some minor legal steps to be taken before our host and hostess apply for the permanent fund.

They also need some help in properly taking the names they now have. Any local attorney could do it, but why have to explain to someone else? Along with that, someone needs to work with the witness protection people to bring them up to date. This new identity won't cost the government anything in moving expenses anyway and they can maybe get the social security numbers squared away somehow for them."

Then he told me that he was glad to get out of San Diego and his poker nights. It seemed that a police detective friend was showing up at every game wearing a hat and sweat shirt from the Red Dog Saloon in Juneau. I suggested that maybe the thing to do was to buy similar items for himself and wear them while not saying anything. As we went back in to the party, he asked me if a mime in court has a right to remain silent. I replied, "Yes, but he is allowed to make a motion."

Later, back on my boat, I thought, "All's well that end's well - but does anything in life ever really end?"

AND THEN

On the day of the informal meeting, the technician who ran the photo processing equipment in the shop at the Emporium Mall was resuming his normal work when he noticed that the machine had been set to print two copies of whatever the police officer had been developing and printing. Only one copy had been taken. He removed the second set and was preparing to call the officer when he glanced at the photographs. Two of the people in the pictures were recognizable; one had left the shop earlier and one was often seen on the news and in the newspapers. He put the phone down and started thinking.